SLEEPING CUTIE

TANZANIA GLOVER

Cover Art by Bree Taylor Design

www.tanzaniaglover.com

I dedicate this to any woman who feels less than "normal". One day you'll come to appreciate what makes you different and I sincerely hope that day begins today.

To my Mommy. I love you more than I could ever say!

PREFACE

Okay so this one still isn't novella length either, but I am getting better with length and time so I'm not complaining. The next one will definitely be a novella though. I'm serious this time.

Also before you guys begin, please note that while this is a continuation of Thickerella, it's a completely different story with a very different set of people so their story will look nothing like Tillar and Cam's.

My intentions for this particular fairytale were to tell a story about navigating the world as a disabled black woman and to highlight how all men (in this case black men) perform misogyny and how they can be accountable for and change themselves.

Enjoy and don't forget to check out the carefully curated playlist that complements this magical tale!

5

1

I'LL SLEEP WHEN I'M DEAD

I was living proof that sometimes the third time wasn't the charm. If my parents would have aborted me when they had the chance then my mother Carolyn would still be alive and my father Cameron would still be happy with his beautiful wife and two sons. But because of me, my dear old dad became a young widower and my brothers Cam and Chase didn't have a mother anymore. To my knowledge he had never treated me any differently from them, but sometimes I could tell that it hurt to look at me because everybody always told me I looked the most like her.

They were given ample warning to get rid of my big headed ass because her body hadn't completely healed from her first two back-to-back pregnancies, but since they'd went from being told that they would never have kids at all to three pregnancies in three years, of course they decided to allow themselves to be led by Faith. The only problem with that was Faith's cousin Fate had different plans for our family and her mean ass decided that my mother would die and that I would live.

Because of that I wasn't sure what I believed and despite my full name being Christian, I had never once genuinely prayed to a higher power. How could I when He'd allowed me to take my mother's life from her?

I had never admitted those thoughts out loud though because the Logan family was big on Jesus and tithing and other shit like that especially my Gram. She was one of those old ladies with the big church hats and the endless supply of peppermints that looked forward to hearing the good word so I didn't let my cynicism stop me from making sure that she was in those pews on time every Sunday. And I always had cash on hand to give her to put in the collection plate even though I knew the whole thing was a sham.

But even with that being said, it was still my pleasure to go with her because with my hectic schedule it was sometimes the only sincere moment I had with somebody for the entire week since I spent my days lying and exaggerating about money better known as investment banking. Taking her to church was one of the many responsibilities that had fallen on me since my dad died early last year from heart disease and we had to put her in a nice home for the elderly.

Chase and I had more than enough space for her then and practically begged her to move into our old place in Harlem, but she insisted on going even though we assured her that she wouldn't be a burden to us. Her response still made me laugh every time I thought about it because she let us know that despite us thinking we were grown that *we* would in fact be the burden on *her* because we both still had a lot of growing up to do.

"I spent my whole life raising kids. These last few days, I want to be with the grown folks."

That was last year though and so far everything had been going as good as it could've been since we had lost the head of the family and really the only thing that was holding everything together.

After that Chase's codependent ass had moved to Brooklyn with his girlfriend so he wasn't too far from where I lived now in Manhattan, but I still barely saw him anymore because his new restaurant was always packed for brunch on the weekends and he hardly ever made it to service anymore. And instead of coming back home to help out with the aftermath of my dad's passing Cam had just further ran off to Atlanta to be with some fat bitch he'd met while living in Chicago.

And now in the third month of spring they were getting married and I had to be there with a smile on my face like I actually gave a damn which I didn't because it wasn't like I was the best man. Like a hard slap in the face, Chase and I had been relegated to simple groomsman like some of the barbers Cam had met at his shop that he had modeled after our dad's.

Personally I thought it was foul to have two alive and well brothers and not make at least one of us the best man since I was all about appearances, but nobody was really surprised to see that he'd picked our cousin Reese to be the best woman since they had been tight since diapers.

I wasn't too pressed about it though because while technically Irish twins with us both, Chase obviously liked me more than Cam so I would definitely get the best man honor when he got married. Plus our rivalry with him had been going on so long that it was hard to pinpoint an exact cause, but for me it went back to Cam getting his own room and Chase and I having to share. Things only intensified when Cam got his girlfriend Summer pregnant.

Gram had scared us for years about the dangers of having sex and disappointing God, but my dad was more realistic and gave us condoms once we got to high school. Because of that I thought for sure that they would shit bricks when

I overheard a sixteen year old Cam telling them that Summer was expecting. The whole thing shocked us all because everybody assumed that Chase was the only one fucking back then since Cam acted like a saint. But before they could even react he said they'd decided to get married and instead of getting punished he was practically rewarded for his mistake.

My dad gave him access to his trust so that he could get a little starter house and car for his new family. Then he opened up another shop location for Cam to run when he turned eighteen. He got everything first. He had the most time with our mother. He got my dad's name. He was the oldest and the tallest. Real talk I just hated everything about him because deep down he wasn't shit either. He just pretended better because nobody was that good.

He was the type of nigga that didn't even want to sneak snacks in the movie theater. He literally paid full price for that shit every time. Chase wasn't much better sometimes, but he still wasn't as bad as Cam. But he still wasn't as smart as me when it came to women and every now and then he would let some female play him too. I'd warned him about the newest girlfriend Parker with the kid, but he would learn the hard way that single mothers were the worst. Not only did they want you to take care of them, but they also wanted you to raise their little bastards too. But I digress.

Watching Cam hand over his nuts at such a young age let me know that I wasn't cut out for married life especially not with the first girl I fucked so I vowed to forever stay strapped even though it wasn't something I had to worry about until much later. Both Cam and Chase always had girls all over them, but Cam only loved Summer and Chase was a serial monogamist out the gate starting with his first girlfriend in middle school. I was less lucky in that department because my looks then left a lot to be desired.

Our whole family was blind as bats and wore glasses, but I was the only one who needed bifocals. I was also tall and lanky with braces and bad skin. It wasn't until the summer before I left for college that I finally came into my own. My braces were removed, my skin finally cleared, I got contacts, and I'd started running and lifting weights so I didn't look like a stick anymore. Basically I became the male equivalent of a bad bitch back then, but it was too late for the girls who already knew me. I pretended like I was Mike Jones because they'd had their chance and they blew it. All I wanted to do then was focus on making money so I wouldn't have to depend on my dad for a check for the rest of my life like Cam did.

Growing up in Harlem, of course I had heard about men like Rich Porter, Azie and Alpo. I knew I wanted to be rich and fly like them, but I wasn't a street dude at all and my dad would've beat the black off of me if I dared try to be one so I had to make it happen with my brain. I was probably the least smart out of the three of us, but numbers were always my thing and anybody who knew them like I did would be a fool to not make money from them. They spoke to me in a way that people never could so it only made sense that I would go on to get degrees in finance and accounting.

On the advice of my dad I'd went to his alma mater Howard along with Chase for undergrad, but making the decision on my own to go to Princeton was the best thing to ever happen to me because it was where I really honed my skills and set my sights on banking. Chase had gotten into Brown, but after a semester there he dropped out to go to culinary school because food was his real passion. The only issue was that he had a problem with authority and didn't like the hazing and racism aspects of the industry so he decided to open up his own joints. The food was always great, but over the years they all kept getting shut down for one reason or another. I admired his resilience though if nothing else. That nigga said he was gonna cook food for the masses or die trying.

But unlike Chase I didn't care too much about being a token at work because it got me to where I wanted to be financially and I felt accomplished being able to live and work where I did now. When we were kids Gram would take us on picnics in Central Park because it wasn't far from where we lived in Harlem and ever since then I knew I wanted to be able to walk outside my door and see that view. I hadn't been living there for too long yet, but that first night felt like home and the fact that I could jog in the park before work meant that I'd made it since most of my coworkers commuted from Jersey or Westchester. After getting settled, I vowed never to live anywhere else because I wanted to be in the city that never slept until I met my hypothetical maker.

A lot of the guys at work were jealous when I announced I was moving in my building because it was known for its long waitlist and tenants being financially probed, but I was proud that a black man could not just get in but could actually live in the penthouse. Obviously nobody who worked at Reisman, Lewis, & Finestein was broke, but racism still reared its ugly head every now and then. In this case it was because I wasn't supposed to be living like or even better than some of them, but I could because they all had families and wives with expensive habits and kids in fancy preschools and houses in the Hamptons. Meanwhile I only had to worry about myself and it bothered a lot of them to their core.

When I first got there I had downplayed my past and let them think what they wanted about me. They assumed that I was a hardworking neighborhood kid who never stopped grinding so I went along with it and even played it up sometimes even though I had more in common with them than they knew. Of course my family's money wasn't as old as theirs was, but I was still a well off kid with a trust just like them. The bosses tried that black tax, underpaying shit with me for the first few years, but now as a Junior VP I got paid more than most with bonuses because I brought in so much that black or not it would have been insane not to put me in a corner office and keep me laced.

I had heard all about the culture of firms in school, but nothing prepared me for my first day as an intern seeing a managing director doing lines of coke with a diplomat through the glass doors in his office. But that was the least of my worries because as a summer intern, I was forced to work insane nearly eighteen hour days because it wasn't uncommon for somebody to drop off numbers that needed crunching at midnight.

And I would never forget being on the

phone with my dad once when one of the associates stopped by my workspace and ended his request by calling me a monkey. My dad was furious and demanded that I get the guy fired until I explained that all the analysts and interns were referred to that way even though I saw how some gleefully said it to my black ass.

But not airing the place out had paid off in the long run. The long days and nights were still tough as an analyst then as an associate for a few more years, but at least it was worth it for the latter because then I had my own team and was actually able to show that I was capable of running shit.

Things had suddenly taken a different turn in the last few months though when the big bosses began forcing Junior and Senior VPs to take the vacations and personal time that we had been encouraged to skip out on for years. They claimed to want to create a work/life balance, but everybody knew the deal. The *New York Times* had written a sort of exposé on the banker lifestyle and how bad the turnover rate was thanks to suicide and drug and alcohol abuse.

Even though it was true that a lot of the guys were high functioning addicts, the fact was that most people weren't cut out for this life and only a few would make it to the top. Even I had tried coke, Adderall, and a few other things to help me get through those rough years as an analyst, but nothing got me higher than the money so nowadays I kept my nose clean and preferred coffee over coke to keep me awake. To cope with the pressure I did have a nasty cigarette habit and of course the occasional cigar with a client, but I was trying to quit the former.

I may have always felt like I hadn't slept in years, but I ate right, worked out, kept my head clear and a flavor of the month around to keep my balls empty so I had no complaints about work or my life in general. I was all set and climbing the ladder faster than most when my doctor first warned me of the stress done to my body from a lack of sleep over the last decade or so.

"You'll be a good-looking corpse soon if you don't take some time off."

"You think I'm good-looking?" I had asked not taking her seriously at all until a few days ago when I'd collapsed from exhaustion in my office, but I still checked my emails in the ambulance on the way to the hospital because I had a live deal.

I laughed in the face of those who called themselves workaholics when it really just meant staying until seven instead of five. I would be right there with the interns and the analysts until two in the morning most days then back at my desk by nine or ten. The analysts and associates did the grunt work for me, but I double and triple checked their numbers to make sure it was up to my standards. I had too much riding on my live deals and I didn't put it past some lowly analyst to set me up to fail since it would be my ass on the line and they could recover at another firm because mistakes were a part of the learning process.

Before being admitted to the hospital, I had successfully pushed my time off until August because that was when most of the finance industry took a vacation anyway, but now the bosses of my bosses moved it up because they claimed to be genuinely worried about me. Not as a person of course, but as a money maker. They gave me twenty business days off, double what the other guys had, which was just a nice way to say go fuck off for a month then get back here and make us even more money.

They wanted me to sleep, but I had done everything but that since it'd been announced because what the fuck was I supposed to do if I couldn't work for a month?

♔

Whenever the weather wasn't too hot or too cold I would get up early enough so that I could exercise before work. Today was no different even though I'd been instructed to take it easy. I felt fine though and the last couple days of rest at home had me in the mood to get my heartrate up. There was a fitness center in my building and another at work, but I preferred running through the park, better known as New York's backyard, and getting some much needed fresh air to kick off my last day in the office for a while. My assistant Neal kept suits and changes of clothes on standby for days like this and even had tuxes in case I had to go kiss ass at a gala or something after work.

Today I would just be popping in to dot the I's and cross the T's on the final paperwork for the deal I'd been finalizing when I collapsed, but I still wanted to run in there looking like a champion since they had all seen me looking like a chump getting carried out on a stretcher the other day. I was no fool though so I wouldn't wear myself out and end up right back in the same place. No, I would take a brisk walk then pour some water over myself to get the same look without any of the hard work.

I had been lying in bed awake but with my eyes closed thinking about all of this for at least an hour. The warm body that'd been next to me all night was still there when I first rolled over, but when I got up to silence my final morning alarm I realized that she was gone and a furry body was in her place.

My black Labrador knew I didn't play that bed shit so I immediately told her to get down, but she didn't listen and instead just pleaded with me to stay like she somehow knew I would be gone for the weekend. This was why I had named her Keith Sweat in the first place because she was always begging me for something.

I hated taking her to the doggy hotel which was just an expensive kennel when I had to leave town, but Chase didn't like dogs and I didn't know my neighbors well enough to ask them to watch her. Lucky for me my longtime dog walker was available to dogsit this time. She had been acting like she wanted me for a while so she jumped at the opportunity, but I was too close to thirty to still be fucking with girls who could barely drink legally so I ignored it and let her do her job. Plus it seemed like every time I fucked a woman who worked for me, the quality of her services would always suddenly begin to decline which was how I had already gone through six personal chefs in four months. And speaking of the latest devil...

Keith suddenly jumped from the bed and went sniffing by the door, but it wasn't until a few minutes later when I also detected the scent of breakfast foods coming from the first floor kitchen. Kira must've finally been cooking again. She had been ordering in for the past couple days since she refused to leave my side after Chase brought me home from the hospital, but I wasn't complaining because her food wasn't the best anyway. I had just hired her because the way she flirted during her interview told me that I needed more than just a sample of her cooking.

I got dressed then began the long trek from my room to the kitchen and thought that I must've been really tired last night because I always took women to the guest room since my sheets were too nice to be fucked up with makeup or whatever other unnecessary shit they wore. But it was all good because her first time in my bed would be her last time here period.

If I was being forced to stay home for a month, I would not be eating bad food just because she could get my whole dick down her throat. But I would miss that. I thought about letting her do it once more before I left until I got downstairs to find her sitting at the counter wearing my robe and drinking coffee from my favorite mug.

"Hey Sleepyhead. I made French toast and poached eggs for two if you're hungry," she offered in a delighted tone, but I wasn't in the mood to return that energy.

"You know I have to go. Why didn't you wrap it up for me? And why aren't you dressed?" I asked because even though she hadn't been working for me long, she still knew the drill. She left when I did.

"I thought I would stay and have dinner waiting for you when you got home," she harmlessly suggested, but the way she said "home" didn't sit right with me because this wasn't *our* home. It was *my* home. "What do you want because I was thinking chicken piccata?"

"Have whatever you want because I won't be here tonight. I'm going out of town."

"For business or for pleasure?"

"Neither. My brother's wedding."

"Cam's wedding is this weekend? Why didn't you ask me if I wanted to go with you?" she asked with arms tightly crossed over her chest.

"Why would I ask you that? You don't even know him. You barely know me," I told her honestly.

"How don't I know you when we've been dating for almost two months now?" she asked in a huff, but it took everything in me not to laugh in her face.

"Knock it off, Kira. We haven't even been fucking for six weeks yet which is also right around the last time you made something that tasted half-way decent so I'm letting you go." Before I could finish my very factual statement, she'd already knocked over my plate of food and stormed off which startled Keith.

"It didn't look that good anyway!" I shouted

after her lying because I hadn't had homemade French toast in a while. Keith took advantage of the situation and quickly grabbed the food then ran up the stairs after her because she was a sucker for every pretty face I brought in here.

All they had to do was pat her head and she was instantly in love. Too bad for them that it didn't happen for me like that.

Kira stared daggers into the side of my face the whole ride down the elevator meanwhile I was just deciding if I wanted to listen to TI or Jeezy for my run. Sure I could've been nicer to her to thank her for taking care of me the last couple days, but in my twenty-nine years I had found that women were more like kids than they realized. You had to be firm and unrelenting with them otherwise they would always find an opening to pop back up and give you a second chance so I made sure never to leave one.

On our way out of my building, she looked over to say one final thing to me, but the sounds of the city and my music was already too loud and I didn't care either way so I turned and began my run and left her standing there.

I was barely passed the rock formations by the Children's Zoo when I found myself getting winded from that cigarette I'd smoked right before leaving out. Every hour that I was in that hospital bed I'd promised myself that I would quit once and for all, but seeing that last pack on my nightstand when I got home had me wanting to finish it first and now I was paying for it.

I knew when I was washed so I packed it in early then slowly walked back towards the benches from the south park entrance because I would need to catch my breath for a minute before heading over to my Park Avenue office building. On my way in the park I had seen a young black woman lying down on those same benches, but I thought nothing of it because that was far from the strangest shit I had seen in this park. However, when I came back around to take a seat I saw a white police officer with his hands on her shoulders trying to wake her up.

Far be it from me to get involved in some shit that didn't involve me, I contemplated continuing my slow walk by until I saw the cop yell at another black woman who was recording him. I ran over and got in between them and used my breathlessness as a part of the lie I'd quickly come up with.

"Excuse me, Officer. This is my wife and we live right across the street. She was coming to bring me my asthma pump, but her allergy treatments make her incredibly drowsy these days," I told him before leaning down to kiss her cheek to make it look convincing, but she chose that exact instance to finally wake up and our lips met for the first time.

"Just go with it," I mouthed to her with my lips still on hers when I saw her eyes widen like she was about to scream as she surveyed the scene that she'd awaken to. I understood completely because if I had woken up with a stranger kissing me, a cop with his hand on his holster, and a small crowd recording the whole thing I would have freaked out too.

Lucky for us both she remained calm and gave me a convincing peck on the lips before sitting up. It wasn't until then that I realized I knew her. Well I had seen her around because she worked as a barista at the coffee bar in my office building. If I had known that it was the one who always gave me attitude I may have kept it moving, but I digress.

"Baby, tell this officer that I'm your husband so I can take you home and get you back to bed," I instructed her, but she was a natural and had already leaned her head on my shoulder as she repeated my words to him.

"See this is just one big misunderstanding, Officer. My name is Christian Logan and I work right down at Reisman, Lewis, and--" I began, but he interrupted me.

"You're not one of Cameron's boys, are you?" he asked as he looked me over again to see the resemblance between my dad and me.

"Yeah, I'm his youngest, but he actually passed last year."

"I know. My condolences. Your father was a good man. He gave both of my kids their first haircut," he said then voluntarily showed me a picture of his black wife and biracial sons, I guess trying to prove that he wasn't racist. "I wasn't going to hurt anybody. We've just been told to keep the homeless out of these areas because of tourists," he said offering a pretty reasonable explanation, but she decided to push her luck now that she knew we weren't in any danger.

"I was just resting my eyes. Do I look homeless to you?" she asked him as I looked over at her. Of course she looked clean and there was no offensive smell coming from her so it was obvious she wasn't, but he didn't look like he completely bought our excuse either.

"My apologies, ma'am. You folks have a good day and next time try to get some rest at home, please," he told her while sticking out his hand for her to shake, but she just frowned at it so I took it instead and thanked him on her behalf.

"That was mad rude of you," I told her when he had gotten far enough away, but she rolled her eyes at me.

"So was him bothering me in the first place."

"He was just doing his job," I said to her, but

I guess she was done with me because she grabbed her things and left me sitting there confused as she thanked the woman that had recorded the incident in case something had happened to her.

I patiently watched them talk for a couple minutes before they exchanged a brief hug then went their separate ways. I knew I must have been bugging because she had just left without thanking me at all and I had more than just held up a phone to defend her. I literally could have gotten myself killed too trying to help. The thought angered me so I caught up with her to at least get some answers about the whole thing.

"If you're not homeless then why were you sleeping out here, Amber?" I asked finally remembering the name that I always saw on her nametag at work.

"Well Chris," she began, letting me know that she knew me too, "I was minding my own business. How about you try it sometimes?" she asked sarcastically and I didn't understand why she wasn't being grateful when I had literally just stopped her from becoming another police brutality hashtag.

I let it slide though because she was attractive even though she looked like a walking GED. She wasn't the tallest, maybe five seven or eight, but she was still mostly legs, I noted because they and her long braids had both went over the bench's limits. Her skin was the color of the darkest of pecans just like mine. Taking another full look at her I realized that even though we had different features, at a quick glance we did look like we could have been related. And maybe it was the narcissist in me for finding her even more attractive when I saw the slight resemblance.

"You don't work at Bean anymore?" I asked when I realized I had been staring and because she had on a green PetWorld polo instead of the black Bean polo I usually saw her in.

"I have two jobs," she said then looked annoyed that the thought hadn't initially crossed my mind. We were obviously headed to the same place, but she walked ahead of me until we were about halfway there. That's when she suddenly turned around and began speaking to me.

"Wait your pops was Cam Logan the barber? He was a legend around here. He cut everybody's hair. He cut Mike Tyson's hair!" she said sounding impressed and I was surprised since my act of bravery was met with such an underwhelming response, but this apparently did it for her.

"Yeah that's him," I told her because everybody knew that his name was synonymous with the best fade in Harlem. My barber now hooked me up, but my cut had never looked better than when my old man took care of it.

"Why didn't you cut hair like him instead of doing whatever you do on the 42nd floor?"

"I'm a banker on the 42nd floor and that life wasn't for me. My oldest brother followed in his footsteps, but I wanted to pave my own way. Plus I don't do too well with the general public," I told her honestly because I could only be bothered with manners and politeness when I was being paid handsomely for them.

"Tell me about it," she said with plenty of snark. "You're always dumb rude and barking at us over your basic ass black coffee order."

"Yeah sorry about that. I guess that's why they're making me take a month off to relax. You should give me your number. Maybe you can show me how to lighten up because I could use some of whatever's got you comfortable enough to fall asleep out here," I suggested even though I had long elevated my taste in women and sworn off ghetto, around-the-way girls from Brooklyn and Harlem. But I was still a sucker for a natural round ass and she had a nice one despite being slim.

I knew better than to shit where I ate because there were too many women in New York to fuck at work especially since situations like that always ended badly. But I was about to go on a long vacation and I'd saved her life so I figured why not since it would probably make her day and I could use some new pussy when I got back from this sham of a weekend.

"No thank you," she said to my surprise while waving me off and adding more pep to her step again. I kept up with her though then specifically asked if she wanted to go grab a cup of coffee since it didn't matter if I was late or not today anyway. Still no.

"Right you're probably sick of seeing it at work so how about something a little stronger some other time then? Like I said, I'm off for a month and I bet we could have some fun together," I pressed, being much nicer to her than I was to others. She was obviously from the hood so I figured she would be appreciative that I wasn't hollering at her from across the street like she was probably used to.

"I don't think so. I have plenty of fun on my own," she said, but I could see that she wanted to tell me to get out of her face.

"But I just saved your life. You have to," I told her, but it seemed that she was suddenly out of patience with me.

"I don't have to do shit but stay black and die. Have a good day," she said, but it sounded more like *fuck you* no doubt from years of practicing at work. She gave off crazy vibes and had an Azealia Banks aura to her like a lot of the fine Harlem girls that I grew up with, but for some reason the thought of fucking that loud mouth kept me pursuing her for the remainder of our walk.

"What? You got a boyfriend or something?" I asked because that had to be the reason somebody like her would even dream of turning down somebody like me.

"No. And I'm not looking for one either. What about you?" she asked curiously and I knew I'd found my in.

"No I'm single too. No girlfriend," I said honestly even though Kira had thought otherwise just half an hour ago.

"Oh I know no woman would deal with you for too long. I was specifically asking if you had a boyfriend," she said with a tilted head.

"Funny, but look this is your last chance to get with the best thing that's ever gonna happen to you," I said trying to play around with her even though I'd meant every word.

She suddenly stopped in her tracks to turn and look back at me and give me one final onceover. She smiled as she took in all that was handsome about me then slowly stepped towards me. Her lips were within reach of mine and I smelled the distinct scent of something cinnamon on her warm breath. Usually I loathed it, but coming from her it didn't disturb my olfactory senses as much as usual.

"Not even if you paid me," she said before finally heading into the building. I smiled to myself at her sense of humor, but I knew that I was going to make her pay for that and I preferred to do it sooner than later.

Amber glared at me as I passed her headed for the elevators, but I gave her a big toothy grin because just like Kira she had no idea that this was about to be her last day at work too.

I showered, quickly handled the paperwork that I'd come in for, then came back down in a suit to look professional because I had one more task to check off my to-do list now before leaving town.

Amber was now changed into her black polo and was also wearing an obviously fake smile as she talked to a customer. Her eyes narrowed when she saw me get in line, but she pretended to be busy cleaning the espresso machine after she'd handed the woman in front of me her drink.

Her coworker took over the station so I waited and let a few other people get in front of me. I checked the time, but my flight wasn't until the afternoon so I could do this all day. A guy in front of me, clearly one of her regulars, personally asked Amber if she could make his drink and she had no choice but to agree. When she was done with him, I quickly asked if she could make mine too before she could slip away again.

"Sure what can I get you?" she asked me with a tight-lipped smile.

"Just a black coffee, please. You know what? On second thought, how about we try something new today? What would you recommend?"

"I'm not sure. I don't drink caffeine," she said smugly, but I knew she was lying because knowing the menu was practically a requirement to being hired here. But since she wanted to play that game, then I could play it too. And there was no better time because the morning rush had just about cleared and everyone else had already been served.

I ordered one of every drink on the menu then took one sip and sent them each back for one petty reason or another. Her coworker mean-mugged me and offered to make me something instead, but Amber insisted on doing it. She didn't want to give me the satisfaction of thinking I'd won, but I saw tears of frustration welling in her eyes by the time we were on round two. I didn't let that deter me though because it wasn't even about not getting her number now. All she had to say was thank you and it would be over.

"Is there something you want to tell me?" I asked before discreetly pressing record on my phone.

"Yeah. I thought I might die an hour ago, but all you were worried about was taking up for the cop and offering me some of your ashy dick. Not a 'you ok, sis?' or nothing. You're a pathetic, non-tipping, woman-hating, *incel* and instead of buying expensive shoes and suits you need to pay somebody to find out what's wrong with you. Now here, take your black ass coffee and get out of my fucking line and off my dick," she said as she roughly handed it to me with no lid so that it would spill on me.

"Is that it?" I asked when I saw a man come out of the back and catch the tail end of her insults. Looks like I wouldn't even need the recording after all.

"No, how about you go fuck your mother too while you're at it, you piece of shit?" she kindly suggested then nearly jumped out of her skin at the authoritative voice calling her name from behind. I knew my work here was officially done, but I decided to rub in the fact that she was about to be canned.

"Hey now that you're about to be unemployed you'll have plenty of time to have all of that fun on your own. You're funemployed!" I quipped as I grabbed my coffee then headed for the exit. I was almost out the door when I saw that my boss's assistant was calling me.

"Mr. Logan, are you still in the building? Mr. Reisman wants to see you in the conference room before you go."

"The conference room? Are you sure?" I asked because everybody in finance knew what lone, last minute conference room meetings meant and I hoped that I wasn't about to meet the same fate that I had already bestowed upon two people today. If so karma was really working overtime these days.

"Yes, he says it'll just take a few minutes," she said assuring me, but that's what I was worried about because firings in the banking world were always quick and painless, at least it was for the one doing the firing. I reversed and came back through the same doors that I had just confidently passed, only now I wasn't so sure if I too would be leaving with my belongings in tow.

Amber was still being reprimanded by her boss and I could see that I was in her line of vision, but she refused to look in my direction. I still didn't feel bad about what I had done, but my journey back up to the 42nd floor certainly felt a lot different now knowing that it might be my last.

To my surprise Reisman wasn't alone in the conference room, but the other directors and VPs were all filing out one by one. All the guys, even the few who openly disliked me, stopped and asked how I was doing and if I had gotten the cards and flowers sent by their assistants because even though I was still wet behind the ears to the most senior bankers and directors, I still got more respect than others because of my connection to the big guy upstairs, Jacob Reisman.

His baby brother Noah had taken to me as my advisor at Princeton and recommended me for my internship because of how innovative I was in his classes. Ten guys would look at the same problem from the same angle, but I always thought outside the box and came up with a solution that no one ever thought of.

Nobody appreciated the connection more than Reisman though because already at my young age, I could charm any client, corporation, or head of government and I was barely in the big leagues. It was because I was a born salesman and even better than selling my financial advice, I could sell myself. I knew most clients were hesitant to put their money in the hands of a black man, but they were always so intrigued after meeting me that nine times out of ten it ended in my favor.

I was great at golf, tennis and racquetball even though I hated all of them, but I would spend my rare time off travelling to an elite course to get some facetime in with potential big fish clients and to dirty mack on how their current advisors were fucking up and costing them millions. I was the kind of guy you could grab a beer with and no matter how stressed I got under pressure I could keep up a cool façade. I could be advising on billions of dollars just going off of a gut feeling, but I never let them think that I was anything less than in full control. But all of that meant nothing because just like all the others before me, I was now alone with my boss in the dreaded conference room.

Reisman could barely wait until the last guy out had closed the door behind him before the big smile appeared on his elderly face. He probably wasn't too much younger than my Gram, but you wouldn't know it by how active he still was. He joked that I looked good for a guy that was nearly on his death bed, but I assured him that I was just a little dehydrated before and that I was fine now. All of a sudden his tone changed and he leaned in closer to me.

"Christian, you know what this meeting is supposed to be, right?" he asked and I nodded but held eye contact to show him that I would accept my walking papers like a man. "Well it won't be that because I just went to bat for you. I know you're not into the heavy stuff like they're implying and you're a good kid so this medical incident will be the last of its kind," he told me as if he could predict the future.

It was finally hitting me what this was all about. They thought I was lying about being sleep deprived and if somebody with a profile as high as mine had died of an overdose on the job, it would bring even more heat on the industry so it would be smarter to just let me go now. But Reisman knew me better than that and of course he wouldn't stand for me going to work at another firm with all the knowledge of inner workings here so he pulled rank and kept me on with one condition to satisfy all parties. That's what the extra days off were really about. It was just enough time to do a quick bid in a program and kick an alleged habit then I could get back to work without a blip on my record.

I sighed with relief at the realization because I knew that all I had to do now was actually relax for the break because I couldn't even remember the last time I'd taken an aspirin let alone anything illegal. But my relief was short-lived because apparently Reisman had one more condition to me staying on.

"When you come back, I need you to tighten up and show everybody that you're responsible enough for what's coming next," he said sternly.

"How do I do that?" I asked genuinely confused because my work ethic was unmatched and nearly everybody loved me here including the clients.

"You know what I mean. Cocaine might not be the problem here, but the ladies are. You need to look stable and family-oriented more than ever when you come back so use this break to regroup then try to meet a nice girl and settle down. I've taken you as far as I can take you, Christian. It's time you learn that the right woman can get you into rooms that no man ever could."

I wanted to dismiss everything he was saying, but I couldn't because I knew Reisman loved me as much as he could a black kid that didn't belong to him so the advice was coming from a good place. For years the older guys here had loved to hear the stories of my wild escapades and live vicariously through me, but since they couldn't attack my work ethic or the profits I was bringing in, they were clinging to anything, even a fake drug habit and my singleness, as an excuse to not give me more responsibility.

Most of the guys, even the younger ones, were in loveless marriages where they barely saw their wife and kids because of the hours. Some were already on their second marriage, but that wasn't the point. They were still married and that ring signified so much around here. It made even the slimiest of guys seem trustworthy. And since I couldn't bond with them over their dislike for their ball and chain, alimony payments, and their kids' jiu jitsu classes I was being ousted on top of my blackness too I was sure. But I knew I couldn't have anything close to that organically in a month so I resorted to doing the only thing I could do. I lied.

"You know it's funny you bring this up because I've already been dating somebody and it's getting pretty serious."

"You and serious in the same sentence is pretty unbelievable," Reisman said with a chuckle as he got up and prepared to leave.

"Well believe it sir. I may brag about my exploits in here, but I've been keeping her a secret because she's…something special. Almost too good to be true," I said fighting the urge to laugh nervously. "Nothing like any woman I've been with before."

"Well be sure to bring this fine young lady with you to my Sarah's bat mitzvah next weekend. I'm sure Jules will love her," he said about his wife and without thinking I agreed. "What's her name? You know for the place settings and gift bags and every other damn thing that Jules has personalized with my money."

"Her name? Oh her name is um…Her name is Amber," I blurted out as his phone rang and I used it as an excuse to get out of there before I dug myself into an even bigger hole. I could lie about money without even breaking a sweat, but apparently throw a woman into the conversation and I was a bumbling fool.

Before I could even process the huge mistake I'd just made, I noticed a couple colleagues of mine had been conspicuously waiting by the door for me to exit, but they looked confused because there was no security around to escort me out. I put on my normal, cool and confident façade and passed them before heading back into my office to sit because just the thought of me settling down actually did make me want a line of coke, but I had to settle for the bottle of whiskey that I kept behind my desk.

The guys, Kemp and Lewis, didn't even bother knocking before they barged in and took seats opposite of me.

"What did Reisman want with you, Logan?" Kemp asked out of genuine concern for my job. I'd gone to Princeton with the guy and we interned together so we were thick as thieves for years, but Lewis not so much though. He was a Yale guy and thought he was hot shit because his grandfather was the Lewis in Reisman, Lewis, & Finestein.

"Not much. Just to talk," I said nonchalantly before swishing the alcohol around in my mouth for a second then swallowing.

"Come on. Nobody is lucky enough to survive the curse of the conference room. I heard from a reliable source that they were bringing the hammer down on you," Lewis said fishing for details on my possible termination or suspension, but I wouldn't gloat even though I had in fact been that lucky. I'd just let him find out on his own how Reisman had given his old grandad his ass to kiss just to save mine.

In the meantime though, I had a plane to catch and apparently a woman to hire to pretend to be my girlfriend Amber for next weekend. I laughed to myself as I finally exited the building because I had just destroyed the only Amber that I knew, but it wasn't like she would've been a good fit for the job anyway. No, I would need to find a sophisticated woman so I turned to the place where men who wanted sophisticated women on short notice went.

A matchmaker.

2

HOW CAN YOU SLEEP AT NIGHT

Unsurprisingly after getting a career saving lifeline and ruining Amber's day and probably her next couple weeks when she'd be low-wage job hunting, I was in a pretty good mood so I decided to try to make the best of the weekend and actually have some fun after all. I would just worry about my predicament with Reisman when I got back to New York. I picked up Gram from the home and I wasn't surprised to see her dressed in her Sunday's best on a Friday afternoon because she was from the generation that still believed flying on a plane was an event within itself.

The nonstop flight from JFK to Savannah, Georgia was just over two hours and I spent most of it thinking about the last time that I'd spoken with Cam. It was about a week after he had proposed and moved to Atlanta and me being me, I immediately brought up the subject of a prenup because I wasn't trying to share our father's money and legacy with a stranger just because he liked sticking his dick in fat women. I was stunned then impressed that he had already discussed the matter with her until he went on.

"It's fair."

"What's fair to you?" I'd asked before offering to refer him to a lawyer that would put complex stipulations in place for her and covertly remove any hindrances like cheating clauses for him.

"Damn. Can we make it down the aisle before you start planning our divorce?"

"Well somebody needs to," I'd said because he may have only looked back on his late wife Summer with fond memories and rose-colored glasses, but I was there and I remembered how everything really went down.

She was on her way to taking him to the cleaners for his trust money even after he had given her the house and was willing to still fully support her and Cree. And don't get me wrong, I always felt bad that my niece was caught in the middle of that tragic situation, but financially Summer dying was the best thing that had ever happened to Cam and his pockets.

That wasn't the kind of shit you were supposed to say out loud though and I got the memo that he was pissed when he hung up on me. After getting an earful from Gram later that night I apologized to him through text and said how I felt low for even thinking like that. Everything shouldn't have been seen through a financial lens, but the job had me on robot cutthroat mode in every aspect of my life. But this was still a man I was talking to, a man that had been through losing a kid and he had limits too so I apologized. He said that he'd accepted it, but I knew he wasn't fucking with me for real because I only knew that I was a groomsmen when Gram told me to get measured for the tux.

But aside from that I still didn't want to go to the wedding because I didn't want to be around his fiancé Tillar's fat friends and I knew she had them because they ran in packs. Where there was one fat woman, there were always a few others waddling not too far behind. And I mean sure she wasn't a dog in the face and she was attractive enough to be a big girl, but she still wasn't the best. I just hoped that there would be at least one bad, desperate woman there with my name written on her, but I wouldn't hold my breath. Gram was still excited though so I put on my best Joker smile and faked it for her as we deplaned.

I'd texted Reese that morning to confirm that she was supposed to be picking us up, but after stepping outside into the fresh Georgia air it was actually Cam standing there with a sign that said *Ida Mae and co.* Even though I wasn't really up to participating in any of this shit, I was glad to see him driving again because I knew what that meant for him.

"Where's Gram and Chase?" he asked me obviously still with a chip on his shoulder from our last conversation. I had known for months that Chase wouldn't be here, but it wasn't my business to tell so I didn't tell it.

"Chase had an emergency at the restaurant, but he sent his love and this," I said as I handed over the card with his wedding gift. It was just a check that I'd looked at only to make sure that I gave them more, not because I cared but just to show up Chase.

"And Gram?"

"She's in the bathroom. You know she hates going on the plane."

"And you left her in there by herself?"

"She's twenty feet away. Calm down," I said before I finally realized he wasn't alone when Tillar summoned me to the passenger side of the car.

"And where's your gift, young man?" she asked playfully. I thought about telling her that I'd brought cash to pin on her, but instead I let her know that Gram had gotten the really expensive shit from their online registry on me and Chase. "Thank you. You know Cam didn't want any gifts because he says we have everything, but I was not passing up the opportunity to make a registry. Do you know how much I've spent on gifts for my friends? Those bitches owe me."

"I know that's right. Cam better get me a yacht when it's my turn with as much as I've spent on y'all for tomorrow," I said looking at him over my shoulder, but instead of responding to me he turned to Tillar and asked her to go check on Gram in the bathroom and they laughed about her getting stuck there at the ball he'd thrown for her last year.

"Sure. I'll be back to properly meet you after I run go tinkle, Chris."

"Take your time," I said as she gave me a quick hug and a kiss on the cheek.

When she was fully out of the car, I realized that she was just as tall as she was big and her shoes gave her a lift because we were eye to eye. At six-three I was the shortest of my brothers and I liked to think it was because they got breastmilk while I got formula. That's why when I finally decided to settle down, I was gonna make my wife pump that shit by the gallon for my shorties. But none of that breastfeeding shit because her titties would belong to me.

And now that I thought about it that would probably explain why both Cam and Chase were always with big titty bitches. I mean I liked them too, but like I said before a nice round ass trumped everything. Lucky for Cam Tillar had that too. *Hell that and then some*, I thought looking after her in her pink and green sequin jumpsuit, the kind where you had to get naked just to take a piss.

I imagined her letting all that loose on the world and had to adjust myself as I looked after her. Of course she was cute in the pictures I had seen online, but she made much more sense in person and it was hard to keep my eyes off of her. I finally blinked when Cam noticed me watching and gave me a light punch to the gut.

"Ay that's my wife you're looking at," he said proudly with his first smile since he'd seen me.

"Not yet. And I see you're still crazy over big titty, one hamburger away type bitches."

"Watch your mouth."

"C'mon. Be a man. Be toxic for once in your life. You earned it. She's got that fire, doesn't she?" I found myself asking pointlessly because I wouldn't dare touch a woman like that and get hooked like he did. He didn't answer me, but the goofy grin on his face as he watched her disappear into the crowd said it all. "Say less. Just introduce me to the sister."

"Actually it's just her and her brother."

"Right. The one you lumped up," I said because I had nearly forgotten about him getting hurt in the fire at his Chicago shop last year. Around that time I was busy closing an important deal so I didn't really care once they told me he was good, but I knew he had been in therapy for his anger issues because Gram was a busybody and ran all of our business to each other.

"Yo Chris you just touched down. Can you not be yourself for like five minutes?" he asked with a stern hand on my shoulder like my dad used to.

"Alright, but not before I tell you that your face is getting mad full, nigga. You been eating good with that fat girl? I know she's a beast in the kitchen." He just shook his head disappointedly at my language then dropped his hand.

"She's getting better," he said, but I couldn't believe that any of us could end up with a woman who didn't know how to throw down after living with Gram our whole lives and my dad wasn't exactly a stranger to the stove either. I swear I missed that big pan of baked macaroni he made for every function almost as much as I missed him.

"Wait let me make sure I have this right? She doesn't work anymore? She doesn't know how to cook? You're putting her through school and fronting money for her little clothing business? Nigga what is she doing to you, playing with your ass?"

"Fuck outta here," Cam said as he put me in a playful headlock and I could tell he was in a good place because we hadn't horseplayed in years.

"Ay watch the waves," I told him as I got loose then ran my hands over my head and checked my reflection in the side mirror. Still perfect, I thought, but I did need it to be fresher for the wedding pictures. I knew he never went anywhere without his clippers so I would have him do it before everything began.

"Those manufactured ass waves. You need to come to Fade Atlanta to get a real cut," he boasted about his newest shop location.

"Nah we only go to the original Fade over here."

"I can tell. You still sleeping in those tights ass durags and claiming to be Dominican to them uptown girls?"

"Yeah, but maybe I wouldn't need them if I had the pillows you sleep on at night," I referred to Tillar's breasts because I did have to admit that I had looked at her Instagram for longer than I was comfortable admitting. "I really can't believe you're already doing this again. If I was you right now I would be running in there to buy a one-way ticket to Mexico," I joked even though it wasn't a secret that I thought marriage was a scam.

I mean women wanted my last name, but they still expected me to pay for everything and then do their jobs at home too. Maybe one day I would be lucky enough to find a diamond in the rough type of woman who would appreciate the bare minimum that I was willing to give her. You know, cute but didn't know it. A woman like Amber actually, but obviously not her because you could take the rat out of the hood but not the hood out of the rat.

"No cold feet for me. I love Tillar and I'm different with her. But I wouldn't expect your forever single ass to understand that yet," he said neutrally, but it still bothered me that he was the third person to say something along those lines today.

"If you love her so much then why are you still letting her wear shit like that?" I asked in all seriousness, but he chuckled.

"Chris, that's a grown ass woman. She can wear whatever she wants. That's your problem now. You fuck around with little ass girls who do whatever you say until they realize you're not breaking them off any bread regardless," he surmised even though he hadn't met any of my women for years. I fucked real models now not just the kind on Instagram, but I ignored that and brought up something he probably wasn't considering while he let her run wild with all of her business showing.

"Okay say another nigga likes what he sees and he grabs her. Then what?"

"Then I'm fucking him up," he said like it

should have been obvious.

"What if you're not there?"

"He better hope and pray that he's gone by the time I get there," he threatened the hypothetical man and it was my turn to laugh.

"Nigga, you're gonna be Captain-Save-A-Hoe til you die," I said before cleaning it up because even though Cam was a gentle giant, I knew how niggas like him operated over their girl. "I'm not calling *her* a hoe. Just saying I've seen this before. Hell twice before. Whatever happened to the last one? Ashley, right?"

"I wasn't trying to save Ashley. We were both grieving, but I needed more time than she did. She's doing better now. She met somebody too," he said before letting me know that he still checked on her a couple times a year.

"Uh oh. Does Tillar know about that?"

"Of course. I'm an open book with my wife."

"Yeah you're open alright," I said as I finally saw Gram and Tillar coming out of the automatic doors holding hands like the best of friends. She could be so phony sometimes, but I loved that old phony broad more than anything.

Gram took the front seat because she always refused to sit anywhere else so that left me and Tillar in the back where I finally got a look at her ring. I didn't know how I had missed it before because it was huge and looked like Cam had majorly overspent on it, but I guess competing with fingers that chubby, you had to either go big or go home.

A Bryson Tiller song came on the radio and it suddenly reminded me that I'd wanted to ask her if she liked his music because his name sounded just like hers. I wasn't really the R&B guy, but I knew of him because one of the women I'd dated for a little while last year was his stylist and she'd dragged me to a couple local shows to get me out of the house after my dad passed.

"Who are y'all talking about?" Cam asked looking at us through the rearview mirror.

"Just a singer," Tillar answered. "You know he doesn't listen to anything made after 1985," she said to me and I smiled at her because she was actually coming off pretty cool so far.

"I like some nineties R&B," he weakly defended. Just like my dad, he'd adopted the philosophy that CDs were too flimsy and if it wasn't on vinyl then it wasn't worth listening to. They weren't entirely wrong, but I could only workout to Jeezy because I was a dope slinging trapstar whenever I decided to go to the gym.

But thinking about Cam keeping all of my dad's old vinyl records to himself after he passed made me want to embarrass him real quick.

"Hey Tillar, did Cam ever tell you how he used to beat off after watching *America's Next Top*

Model?"

"He used to what now?" Gram asked looking at Cam over her glasses, but he stifled a laugh and focused on the road.

"It's nothing, Gram. He's lying," Cam said denying it, but Tillar didn't buy it because she leaned over and barely whispered to me.

"He didn't, but I figured as much. He's obsessed," she said as she gestured at her chest and I took the opportunity to follow her hand and get another sneak look myself. Shit I could see why.

"Y'all do know we can hear you right? Have some respect for Gram."

"Why are you always acting like Gram hasn't *lived*? You might look the other way, but I know why Deacon Johnson comes to visit her every week at the home. He gives a whole new meaning to speaking in tongues, right old girl?" I asked suggestively before she turned to point her finger at me.

"He stops by to pray for every resident. Now Christian, don't you go gossiping about that sanctified man of God!"

"I don't know. The lady doth protest too much," I said quoting *Hamlet* since she practically had us memorizing it from reading it so much as kids. We all laughed, but I could see Cam was holding back until Gram broke and grinned a little too.

See I always had the more playful relationship with her than he and Chase did. No doubt it was because I worked her nerves the most to the point that sometimes instead of punishment, she just had to laugh at whatever situation the younger knucklehead me had found myself in.

"I'm just messing with you since you run everybody's business. It's about time we did the same for you, old lady. How does it feel?"

"The same as it will feel when I get Cameron to pull over and hand me a switch to put you over my good knee."

"You did that one time my whole life and you haven't done it since."

"She never did it to me," Cam said looking over at her proudly.

"So? I'm still the favorite, right Gram?" I asked, but she was too busy admiring the big house we were approaching from the long, circular driveway.

I knew that they had rented out an estate for the wedding and the reception, but they had neglected to mention that it practically looked like Thomas Jefferson's Monticello home. Tillar laughed at my accusation and claimed that she would never get married on a plantation, but that shit was big and white and in the south so I would be looking in the back for slave quarters before I left.

Cam got me checked in quickly because the rehearsal and dinner was starting soon and I still needed to get my cut fresh for the weekend. Inside the room were three double beds and I could see that his shit was already set up on one of them. Before I could say anything about it he was filling me in as he went to take a piss with the bathroom door still half open so I could hear him.

"There weren't enough rooms and Tillar really wanted her own dressing room to get ready in like she does at home. And I figured you and Chase wouldn't mind me crashing with y'all because we never got to share as kids."

"Don't stunt. You loved not sharing with us because you got to sneak Summer in," I joked but quickly decided to move on to a different subject so I asked him where his clippers and cape was so I could set everything up.

The first things I saw when I opened his suitcase were condoms and a bunch of books. I was almost proud thinking that he carried them because he was cheating on her until I realized what they were really for.

"Ay please don't tell me you're marrying her and you ain't been *all* the way up in that? Shit tell me you've hit period, nigga!" I demanded as he came out drying his hands.

"I actually hit on the first date," he said like he had something to prove to me which was rare. "And not that it's any of your business, but we're not using them anymore after the wedding. I just brought them along in case to make sure she's comfortable," he said sounding like an afterschool special and I disappointedly sighed at him.

"Yo I thought those were her titties at first, but now I know they're actually your balls strapped to her chest," I laughed out, but he didn't join in. "Look all I know is that condoms, books, and a hiking trail map does not say endless fucking to me. What kind of boring, *Little House on the Prairie* ass honeymoon are you having out here?"

"Well I gotta get back to the shop by the weekend and she's got school so we couldn't really go too far. Plus she just wanted to hike since she hasn't been in a while."

"And what about what you want? See this is why I'm never getting married. Everything is all about them. What about us?"

"I want what she wants and she wants to hike," he said simply.

"I can't tell looking at her."

"That's funny, but you got one more of those before I rearrange your jaw and push your lining back, baby brother," he said as he gripped the back of my neck hard then gave me a noogie. I didn't know why he loved pulling that *baby brother* shit when he was barely two years older than me.

And if I'd have known that he would be fucking up my waves, I definitely would have gotten a haircut before I left home, but I didn't because I knew I wanted to talk to him to clear the air from the last time we talked.

"So Gram said you've been in therapy?" I asked after he turned on the clippers and he confirmed it with a nod. "They making you do that for the case?"

"Nah. I just paid my fine for that, but I promised Tillar I would do it if she took me back. It's not that bad and it's actually helping me get some shit out that I didn't know I was still holding in."

"I guess, but I don't really see the point. From what I heard, her brother got out of line and you handled it. She should be thanking you."

"That's 'cause you didn't see him. It was overkill and I got off easy this time. I'm not taking a chance with the law or losing my wife again. What?" he asked when he saw me shaking my head in disbelief.

"Nothing I just see who's wearing the pants down here," I told him because she had him wrapped around her fat ass finger. Even when I did eventually decide to get a ball and chain, I would be the one in charge.

"How about we both wear the pants because I'm not trying to rule over her like she's a kid? What, you want me to call her out of her name or hit her?" he asked and I kissed my teeth at him exaggerating.

"Nobody said shit about hitting her. I'm just saying show her that you're the man."

"Nah. Face it. You're a dysfunctional, bitter nigga and that's why no woman in her right mind would ever put up with you," he said meaning it to be an insult, but I took it as a compliment coming from a simp like him.

"Shit if you can get it, I know I could get it too, but I'm not in the business of getting on my knees to beg a bitch to be with me." I could sense that we were about to clash about our ideologies on women when we were saved by a loud knock on the door. He purposely clipped my ear then went to go answer it. "Ay you ain't shit," I chuckled out before Tillar stormed in ranting about the wedding photographer asking for more money, but she had refused it.

"So what? We'll give it to him then leave a bad Yelp review," Cam joked.

"No. My new phone has a great camera so we'll just make do with that," she said seriously, but he wouldn't hear of it and got his phone out to fix everything with a quick call.

"You really didn't have to do that," she said and I silently agreed with her because as usual he was doing too much.

"Yes I did. What did I say you deserved? C'mon say it, Tills."

"Galaxies. But I'm sick of all of these damn surcharges popping up all over the place so I'm stealing a lamp or something when we leave because they are not getting away with this," she pouted as she headed back out the door.

"I'll take one too. Oh and if anybody calls you about anything else, remind them that they're supposed to call me."

"And why is that, Mr. Logan? What do you have up your sleeve now?"

"None of your business, Mrs. Logan. You'll see tomorrow," he said before she finally acknowledged my presence, but it was only to grumble about city boys as she took my suitcase from the bed and sat it on the floor.

"Aren't you from Chicago?"

"Yes, but I am a southern belle at heart and don't you forget it, Chris. And you, I saw the flowers you had sent to my room. They're beautiful," she said to Cam before planting a kiss on his lips.

"Well it's still Friday, right?" he said and I deduced that he sent them weekly on that day.

He was just setting himself up to fail

though because a man should never start something that he couldn't keep up with. The rule was to always keep a woman's expectations as low as possible, but see Cam got that nurturing spirit from being up under Gram too much as a kid. He cared like women did and that shit always had him with his nuts exposed and his nose open waiting to be taken advantage of. Lucky for me I had rap to turn to because I sure wouldn't have learned how to really treat these hoes at home.

"I don't want to hear it," he told me once she had left. "Yes I got her spoiled and that's how I like it," he said proudly.

"But you literally threw her a ball already. How much do you have to spend to make her happy?"

"You're lecturing me about reckless spending? Look at how much you pay to rent your penthouse just because Madonna used to live there."

"The difference is I can afford it," I said letting my nuts hang some because while he wasn't hurting for money, I was a couple tax brackets above him now and only climbing higher by the day. "And it was Lady Gaga by the way. Not Madonna."

"Same thing. And you must've forgotten that I can afford shit too. But you, you're just working yourself into an early grave and for what? You ain't even got nobody to leave your shit to," he said and instead of coming back with something I just let him think he got the last word since there was no amount of common sense that could reach a nigga as far gone as he was.

The second he finished wiping me down, there was another knock on the door. This time I got up to open it, but instead of Tillar standing there it was Reese and she was looking more dapper than usual because I was sure she was on the hunt for thirsty wedding bitches just like I was.

"Chareese! My nigga! You look handsome," I said as she walked in and I meant it because that's the look she had been going for.

I still couldn't believe that her mother, my Aunty Catherine, really thought moving her away from us back in the day would help her be more feminine since all she did was run around with the boys, but it obviously hadn't worked. Growing up I always felt bad for her having to wear dresses and shit and pretend like she wasn't gay, but after getting to Chicago she shunned all that shit and came out as a lesbian.

"I try. I bet I pull more bitches than you tonight," she wagered holding up her wallet and I accepted whatever amount she wanted to put down.

"Y'all are mad childish," Cam said, but I

ignored him because I already saw something that had caught my eye on the way in so I called dibs to let Reese know to stay out of my way.

"The wedding planner? Nah that's all me. I got the strap waiting on her in the room," she said and I frowned at the thought.

"Hear you go again making niggas uncomfortable talking about your weak ass strap game," I said before I was finally ready to head down and get this night over with.

The two families were officially introduced before the rehearsal and rehearsal dinner started and I was surprised to see that Tillar's side mostly consisted of friends. Gram had already given me the scoop that her aunt would be walking her down the aisle since her father had passed years ago and her mother wouldn't even be in attendance. I didn't have to fish for more details because Gram volunteered that she had recently relapsed and was in a program for alcoholics.

Just like I had suspected, Cam had picked another damaged woman with a troubled background. She was just like Summer and Ashley only bigger.

Since Chase wasn't here, I would walk down the aisle with two bridesmaids by my side, but I couldn't even use it as an opportunity to flirt because one was Tillar's married cousin and the other was her teenaged niece. Her family must have been Amazonians because I had only ever seen women their height on a college basketball team.

The rehearsal ran smoothly and was over in the blink of an eye and I was thankful because the whole time I smelled the barbecue on the grill that was being served for dinner tonight and I couldn't wait to get a plate. The drinks had me feeling nice and I was enjoying laughing with everybody until Reese decided to do a practice run at her speech because it once again reminded me that Cam hadn't picked me for the job.

"I gotta be serious for the real speech tomorrow so I'mma get these jokes off tonight then make everybody cry tomorrow. I bet everybody here knows Cam's simp story about how he met Tillar at the barbershop, but what most people don't know is that I was supposed to cut her hair that day so allow me to set the scene. A'ight so boom. Shorty walks in. Of course off rip she's all on me. But I'm like 'Nah. You're bad, but my mans over here will appreciate you more--'" she said before Cam interrupted her and the laughs began.

"None of this happened by the way."

"It did. I told her. 'He'll be good to you. He may not be as handsome as me and my cuts are better, but—'"

"Oh now you're crossing the line," Cam said

as he playfully stood up and took off his jacket.

"Alright. Alright. The point of that was to tell Tillar that this could've been us, girl."

"It's still not too late!" Tillar said making everybody laugh.

"But all jokes aside, I saw my cousin through some of his darkest and his lightest times, but I ain't never seen him shine like he does when he's with you. You've been Fade Family Gang, but I want to welcome you to the Logan Gang for life," she concluded and was met with lots of applause and even a few tears from Tillar and Gram. I clapped too because it was a decent starter speech, but I would've had my assistant Neal write a better one if I was up there.

Once we had gotten the clean fun out of the way it was time to separate everybody by age because the next part of the night wasn't fit for kids or elders. There were two big rooms for entertainment and one was being used for the joint bachelor and bachelorette party. When I heard they were doing it together, I was disappointed that I wouldn't get to go to a famous southern strip club, but once all the hoe friends who weren't in the wedding party started showing up I knew for sure that I wouldn't be ending my night with a full sack anymore.

About halfway through the night I saw Reese stepping outside to go smoke so I wasn't too far behind her. The scent of some good but stinking weed was already permeating the air that I walked into on this humid Georgia night.

"Gram's gonna kick your ass if she smells this shit on you."

"She won't," she assured me as she pulled out a little bottle of Armani cologne to mask it, but it just smelled like Armani made a weed fragrance now.

I hadn't smoked weed since undergrad, but I was in need of some relaxation after the day I had so I took a hit then gave it back. She looked up at me then complimented my cut before asking why I didn't get her to do it instead of Cam, but she knew good and well that she wasn't allowed near me with a blade ever again.

"I think I made the right choice, *Edward Scissorhands.*"

"Yo you still on that? We were shorties when that happened!" she laughed out like she didn't leave me wearing an eye patch for months after dropping a razor on my cornea.

I'd begged my dad for weeks to let me get cuts in my eyebrows after seeing Soulja Boy with them. He agreed once I proved it wasn't associated with any gangs, but he told me to wait so he could do it himself. Of course I didn't.

The whole thing was my fault though because I was sixteen at the time and I should have been done following rapper trends by then anyway. As a preteen Nelly had me using up all the Band-Aids from our first-aid kit and TI had me wearing rubber bands on my wrists. Nobody could judge me though because it was the early two-thousands and it was a different time then.

We weren't even supposed to be listening to music like that at all, but I needed all the help I could get trying to fit in so I would wait til everybody went to sleep then sneak to the den to download music from Limewire. I retitled everything because Gram would tear my ass up if she knew all that Fred Hammond I was listening to was really Lil' Wayne and that Kirk Franklin was actually 50 Cent.

I was a proud crew hopper then too. One minute I was a St. Lunatic then I was screaming Wangsta with G-Unit. Thank god those days were over with now because I didn't even try to keep up with this new shit. I only had one tattoo and I didn't care what new weirdo hairstyles became popular or if those lumberjack looking beards were a thing again. My waves would forever be on swim and I kept just enough facial hair to avoid looking like a baby in the face.

"I'm glad you still think that shit is funny. I had to get a second round of Lasik because of that a couple years ago," I said which just made her laugh harder.

"Look I was practically grown as hell, but Gram still beat my ass with a belt for you that day so we're even."

"I think me looking like Slick Rick for months was enough of an ass whooping, don't you think?" I asked before we fell into reminiscing about all the other funny shit we had done as kids and teens.

"Man I can't believe Chase didn't come. I'm busting his ass next time I go home," she said referring to Harlem as home even though she had lived in Chicago longer now.

"Nah you know he's not letting shit mess up this new restaurant. Gram can't even make him come to church down the block so you know he wasn't leaving the state."

"He would've done it for you," she said sounding like Cam's little helper, but I didn't care because she was right. Me and Chase had each other's backs just like they did.

"Nah he didn't want to see me scoop up the maid of honor Nicole," I bragged because I had seen her looking at me a few times throughout the night.

"You really going in there after your brother?"

"Wait Cam hit that?" I asked impressed because maybe there was a little dog in him after all.

"Man hell no. Chase," she said before letting me know that it'd happened last year after the ball. It was news to me though because he hadn't said a peep about it to me. "My bad. I thought he still told you everything."

"Nah," I said simply then changed the topic to let her know that her and Cam's relationship wasn't perfect either. "So how does it feel now that he left you too?" I asked, but she waved me off.

"He's doing good down here. Give her a chance. Tillar is good people and she's good for him."

"Nah I know she's cool. Cam's just still on his usual Mr. Perfect shit trying to make everybody around him settle down. He still getting on you too?"

"Of course. But every time I tell him that I'm not getting married until the hoes stop calling," she said which all of a sudden got me to thinking.

Cam always claimed that he didn't like the way me and Chase treated women, but if that was really the cause of the strain in our relationship then shouldn't that have also extended to Reese? I mean yeah she was a woman too, but it was the exact same behavior.

Before I could think too hard on it, Cam had came out to collect us or Reese rather so he wouldn't be by himself in there. He liked to stay low so I knew that kind of crowd was overwhelming to him. I was usually the life of the party, but I wasn't feeling up to it tonight for some reason. I just wanted some pussy and to take my ass to sleep because I was running on fumes now.

"Yo you're doing it!" Reese said excitedly as she grabbed Cam's shoulders. "This time tomorrow you're officially out the game again."

"When has this nigga ever actually been in the game?" I asked her, but he answered instead.

"Never and that's how I like it. Shit I barely want to leave the house alone anymore. The women down here...man they're different. The bank teller tried to give me her number the other day with Tillar right next to me," he complained as we headed back inside, but I didn't see the problem in making women compete because it kept them on their toes.

I knew he wasn't lying about the boldness of women in Atlanta though because I'd already seen that some of Tillar's single friends were on the lookout for eligible and ineligible men from the way they were looking at both of us. Cam didn't go to college so he didn't know the culture like that, but I had seen it all at Howard and I knew that all of this skee-wee-ing sorority shit they were doing was just a front for freak hoe behavior.

And the sea of pink and green hoe clothes dancing around was all the evidence I needed to reaffirm that belief. Not that I was complaining, but who wore shit like that to a wedding event? But I guess they were just following Tillar's lead because her breasts and ass were on full display and I could finally see why Cam was marrying her as she bent over to do a move with her line sisters because backshots from that thing had to be ungodly.

"And you still want to get married?" I asked him again looking at the platter of attractive women in front of us, but he just smiled and looked at the one in front.

"More than ever. And I just wanna know what I did to deserve her so I can do it again in my next lifetime," he said before going over and pulling her out of the line so that he could have her to himself.

That was the last thing on my mind though. After my fourth or fifth drink and finally feeling the effects of Reese's blunt, I was ready to fuck then hit the sack. I'd seen Reese playing the rounds and talking to the wedding planner Leah and a few others to better her odds, but I took advantage of a bathroom break and swooped in for the kill. Even though she seemed more interested in Reese, she had still been eyefucking me across the room all night so I wasn't surprised when she followed me after I walked up to her and asked if she was ready.

I knew I couldn't take her back to my room because of Cam and I also didn't want to go to whatever hotel she was staying in because I would be stuck spending the night there since I was in no condition to drive nor was I getting in an Uber after dark in Georgia. But I had seen a big coat closet near the entrance that was unused because nobody would ever need a coat in May in hot ass Savannah. I grabbed her hand and ducked inside then flicked off the lights.

"Well aren't you romantic?" she said sarcastically even though her arms were already wrapped around my neck and she'd lifted her leg for me to hold onto.

"You don't have to front for me, Leah. I know that romance is the last thing on your mind because tonight all you want is for a man to hit a spot that probably hasn't ever been hit and leave you satisfied enough to do your job with a real smile tomorrow," I said reading her how I did clients at work.

And with as much bravado as I'd had during my impromptu speech, I was sure that I was about to beat it out the frame, but after about ten minutes of kissing and touching, we weren't getting anywhere because I couldn't mentally get myself ready. I wanted to blame it on the drinks, but even when I had been nearly blackout drunk before my guy was always trained to go. I sighed because I felt her getting frustrated at all the work she had put in for nothing.

"Fuck. I don't know what's going on, but this literally never happens," I explained, but she just put her titties back up and pulled her dress down and left me standing there.

"I knew I should've chosen the stud. Her dick stays hard," she mumbled to herself as she left the closet.

I sat on the floor behind an empty coatrack for a few minutes because I was embarrassed at what'd happened. Again I was drunk but not that drunk so I knew it had to be something else. I stupidly entertained the idea of Amber at home right now hexing my dick. I laughed to myself until I heard voices from right outside. It wasn't until the door was open that I recognized them.

"What do you have to show me in here?" Cam asked before being dragged inside by a tipsy Tillar and I knew that she must have had the same idea as me.

"Shh. It's a surprise," she said before stumbling over the same hanger that Leah and I had just tripped on.

"Slow down. You don't wanna be hungover for your wedding day, do you?"

"Oh I plan on being drunk off my ass then

too," she laughed out.

"Not me. I want to remember everything," he said and before he could finish his sentence, she was already slobbing him down and working on unbuttoning his pants until he stopped her.

"You're really still making me wait? This penis belongs to me, Mr. Logan," she slurred.

"Are you forgetting that it was your idea for us to wait this week, Mrs. Logan?"

"Yeah, but I was doing just fine before you snuck into my room with the munchies last night."

"That's because I had a sweet tooth and I was missing my *midnight snack*," he told her even though I thought a *buffet* seemed more accurate, "but we made it this far so we can wait one more day."

"Fine. I'll go have fun by myself then," she said with her hand on the doorknob, but he pulled her back into him.

"We still on for tomorrow?" he asked playfully as if the wedding would be their first date or something.

"Mm…maybe. I've got to check my calendar first."

"Yeah it's a date. And do you realize that in a few minutes, it'll be exactly one year to the day that I told a shop full of customers that you would be my wife?"

"Of course I remember. That's why I chose this day, silly."

"That's not the point. You didn't believe me back then, did you?" he asked and she shook her head no. "Well how about now?" he asked with a big grin before he went on.

"Tills, I can't wait to promise to love you for better, for worse, for richer, for poorer, in *thickness*--I mean in sickness and in health," he joked as he ran his hands down and palmed her ass cheeks which just seemed to reignite her previous mission. I couldn't see what she was now doing to him, but whatever it was made him groan and curse so I knew I had to get out before I ended up stuck while they did what I couldn't get done with Leah.

"Wait before y'all start, let me out."

"Chris, what the fuck?" a startled Cam yelled at me as he covered Tillar up. "What are you doing in here? You a voyeur now?"

"That's a dumb question. If I was a voyeur I wouldn't have stopped you, would I?" I slurred some as I tried in vain to get up which garnered a small laugh from Tillar.

"Oh lord. I'm going back to my party. Go help your brother to your room before he gives somebody else a heart attack," she said before turning on the light then leaving us alone. Cam just looked down at me and shook his head before helping me up.

"My bad. I was just trying to get a minute away from all that phony shit, but I'm still telling Gram you got drunk and dry humped in a closet."

"Give up. No matter what I'm always gonna be her favorite," he said, but before he could get it out I projectile vomited all of that good barbecue from earlier all over the floor. He had gotten out of the way before any could get on him so he didn't even trip and just said he would clean it up after he got me up to our room.

After he got me in bed and took off my soiled shirt, he asked if I needed anything. I told him I needed another drink because the water he'd already given me wasn't helping to wash that disgusting taste from my mouth.

"I think you had enough for tonight, baby brother," he said before telling me he was going back down to the party, but I wouldn't let him off that easily.

"Then maybe you should have another so you can finally get enough liquid courage to admit the truth about why you really don't fuck with me," I began before letting him know he was a hypocrite since Reese treated hoes the same way I did.

"And why is that?" he asked sounding amused until I answered.

"Because of what I did to Ma."

"Yo you're bugging! It can't be because you're immature and you use and disrespect women, right? It has to be over something you know you had no control over? You know even when you're dead wrong you're still always trying to escape accountability. That's the reason why I don't fuck with you, Chris!"

"What about Chase then? That nigga stays loving bitches in a relationship and you know he lowkey envies you," I asked and just saying Chase's name seemed to upset him.

"Chase? You mean the nigga that wouldn't even get on a plane to be here for me today? That Chase? And y'all wonder why Reese will be standing up there next to me tomorrow. From the bottom of my heart, fuck both of you selfish motherfuckers," he spat in my direction as he got in my face.

"You want to know why I'll always be the favorite? Because I actually listened to the shit Gram and Dad told us and even when I make mistakes I fall in line and correct that shit. You niggas don't know shit about that though and that's why I'll never fuck with y'all."

"Ay get out my face with that tough nigga shit when we both know you're softer than baby shit," I said daring him to do something as I pushed him and as expected he put his hands up in surrender and backed off.

"You need to get a therapist like everybody else and get over yourself, Chris. It's after midnight and I'm not letting your shit fuck up my wedding day," he said over his shoulder as he headed for the door.

I always felt big except when I was around Chase and Cam even though everything about me was a façade even down to my muscles. I had never even been in a fight in my entire life because everybody knew that my brothers had learned how to box from our dad so they never really bothered me by default. Nowadays my height and voice were intimidating, but admittedly my bark was much bigger than my bite because I still wasn't a fighter at all.

Still I was drunk and wanted to give it a try for a change, but I wasn't so drunk that I didn't contemplate if it would be a good decision or not. See Cam had learned early that his hands were dangerous and kept them to himself unless it was necessary. He had knocked some big high school nigga out cold in middle school then cried right after because he didn't like fighting or hurting people. He had only did it to protect me though because Chase could always handle himself. I'd missed those days, but I knew they were never coming back with what I was about to say.

"Why?" I asked hoping to bait him back in because he was almost out the door.

"Why what?" he asked after a sigh.

"Why do you care if the wedding is fucked up? It's not like it's your first one and it probably won't be your last since you're still too boring for even her fat ass too," I said to his back expecting him to keep walking away, but instead he quickly came back over and hand delivered that two-piece with no sides that he'd promised me earlier.

I thought he'd punched me as hard as he could in the jaw until I felt his left fist connect underneath my right eye. That's when I swear I saw my life flash before my eyes and I went limp. My ego told me that he'd gotten me in the full Nelson because I was too drunk for my reflexes to really kick in, but I knew the truth. This nigga still had hands and it looked like I'd gotten him pissed enough to finally use them on me.

His forearm suddenly loosening the chokehold that he had me in brought me back to the present after he tossed me on the floor like a used napkin. He was breathing hard and could barely get words out, but I couldn't do shit but lay there so I heard them loud and clear.

"You don't know how lucky you are that my wife is nearby and that therapy actually fucking works. Otherwise I would dogwalk your little ass in here. And after tomorrow you don't ever have to say shit else to me, Chris, but you better be in formation like Beyoncé with the rest of the groomsmen in the morning or I swear to God you're leaving Georgia in a body bag," he threatened and even though I knew he wouldn't actually kill me, I knew that he would kick my ass again and I wanted no more parts of that.

"Alright. Just don't tell Gram about this. Please," I begged him as I tried to get up, but I felt a sharp pain in my side. Nigga must've hit me there too.

I laid there for a while until I didn't hear music anymore or anybody else's passing footsteps before finally stumbling back to the bed. I was almost scared to sleep lest I wake up the beast again, but just like I figured he didn't even come back. He'd probably gone to cry on Tillar's big titties and I wished that I could do the same because he had hit me so hard that even the soft pillows on the bed weren't enough to sooth the pain I was in.

I barely got any shut eye, but the little that I did manage to get was interrupted by Gram opening the curtains to let the near blinding sun in then putting an ice pack on the side of my face because apparently Cam's bitch ass had told on me after all. She didn't even bother going off on me about what I'd said this time. She just told me to get up and get dressed because we were going to have a blessed and joy filled day no matter what. And she was right because no matter what, everything Gram said was law.

Cam showed up to the room right after I'd gotten out of the shower, but he wasn't by himself. Nicole was with him and she had a small makeup bag with her. She officially introduced herself to me then said she'd heard that I bumped into a big door last night and that I might need a little cover up for the pictures. I smiled to myself at what they were calling Cam's fists then let her work on me. Cam didn't even pretend like he was there for anything but to make sure she was comfortable being in a room with me by herself for those few minutes.

I understood because I was a stranger to her, but it still hurt that my own brother didn't trust me enough to vouch for me, but I guess I had myself to blame for that because I didn't have the best track record with laying out the red carpet for the opposite sex. Still he should have known me better than to think I was a danger to them.

I took one last good look at Nicole before she left to try to see what had attracted Chase because aside from the long hair she was way smaller than his usual type. But I guess it really didn't matter what she looked like because he probably just wanted to get with her since Tillar didn't have any sisters, but she still got him one degree closer to double dating with Cam.

I knew that this was the last time I would

have his ear to apologize before the chaos of the wedding began, but I didn't want to do it in mixed company so I just let him walk out then got dressed. It wasn't too long later when Reese showed up to let me know that everything was starting.

The outdoor area that was set up for the wedding ceremony looked like a winter wonderland when I made it out back, a direct contrast to the night before. And since nobody had mentioned a themed wedding during the rehearsal yesterday, I knew this was the surprise Cam had for Tillar. Reese confirmed my suspicions when she said that Tillar had always wanted a winter wedding so Cam decided to bring the snow to her.

The cleanup would be a bitch since it covered every inch of the land, but it was just one more reminder of how much he loved her. And for the first time I realized that maybe some of the pity I felt towards my brother for always being so lovesick was actually jealousy because it was one more thing that he had gotten before me. I mean no woman had ever inspired me to do even half of the shit that his goofy ass did and I knew that being with me had only caused women to question their choices and their common sense.

It wasn't until then when I realized that I had never actually imagined myself being in love.

Married, yes, but in love was a completely different conversation. And whenever I pictured that kind of commitment for myself, it was always a much older version of me because I knew I had plenty of time to get to that next stage in life.

But maybe I'd been mentally pushing it off because at least for the foreseeable future, I couldn't imagine a woman actually wanting to marry me for me. Not my checkbook or my looks, but just for me. I guess that was why I had learned to get rid of them before they could get rid of me. And even when they did leave me first, it was only because I had pushed them to it.

Watching Cam's already teary eyes as he excitedly watched Tillar's double in size when she began walking down the aisle was a sight to see. And simply put, she looked beautiful. And she was still marveling over all of the surprise snow when the stars began to fall from the sky.

Everybody instinctively looked up to see a small plane releasing hundreds of thousands of what looked like little white snowflake stars from above.

"Mr. Logan! No, you didn't!" Tillar said as she closed her eyes.

"I did Mrs. Logan. I'm giving you the galaxies," he said before the tears that'd welled in his eyes began to fall along with the remaining stars.

Seeing men cry at their weddings was something I'd never understood before. Like nigga, you knew this day was coming so just stop it with the nonsense. But seeing my brother cry tears of joy as he recited his vows and promised to love and protect his new wife until there was no more breath in his body even got me a little choked up even though I wanted to blame it on that shot I'd taken to help my hangover.

That shit was just mad inspiring though and there was so much love in the air when they jumped the broom that all of a sudden I could hardly breathe because I knew that it would never be like that for me if I didn't do something drastic to get out of my own way.

After I had fake smiled for the pictures and listened to all of the toasts, I retreated back up to my room because I didn't feel up to keeping up the act anymore. I was tired and the pain medicine I had taken earlier was wearing off so I needed a quick re-up. I undressed then got back in bed to finally put some thought into what I would do when I got home about Reisman's party and the Amber stand-in that I now needed.

Just thinking of her name made me remember that I had been meaning to look up the word *incel* ever since she'd shouted it at me the other morning. I was immediately confused because the first few things that came up in my search were news articles about radicalized men who had stalked, hurt or even committed mass murders specifically targeting women. Of course that sounded nothing like me especially when I saw that their crimes were motivated by them being **in**voluntarily **cel**ibate, hence the name.

I started to put my phone and the crazy notion that I was somehow an incel away because I hadn't been involuntarily celibate since high school. But the more I read on, I saw that I indeed had way too many similar beliefs about women with those extremists and it made me uncomfortable because I would never hurt a woman or anybody for that matter.

That was one of the few things that I'd carried with me from my dad. He had been dead and buried for over a year now, but I still believed that he would somehow wake up from his grave, dust himself off then square up with me if I even thought about laying a finger on a woman.

And besides, if prioritizing financial success and not being a hopeless romantic meant that I was an incel then so was every man I knew because *Fuck bitches, get money* were words to live by, but with my latest revelations I knew it went deeper than that so I stopped pretending immediately.

I had been called a lot in my day. *Cheap. Trifling. Hoe.* But I took pride in those labels. It was what I aspired to. *Incel* was legitimately an insult though and if a stranger could see something like that in me so easily then I needed to make sure that nobody else could. Hell maybe that's where Reisman's straightforward advice about me settling down had come from. I was sure he wouldn't call me an incel, but him saying that I needed to be more family-oriented when I returned to work was basically in the same ballpark.

Then Cam's words from the night before sounded off in my head and I started wondering if he had a point too. I mean what really was the point in having all of my money and things if I had nobody to share it with or even pass it on to? Both him and Chase were serious and partnered up and I had nobody. I had just been in the hospital and if it wasn't for the chef that I was fucking, I literally wouldn't have had anybody to look after me unless I paid them.

As I laid there looking up at the ceiling, it hit me that in the past twenty-four hours Amber and then Reisman and then Cam had all been right with their assessments of me and I may have actually been a fucking incel.

I'd spent so long trying to do the opposite of Cam and men like him that I never stopped to see if any of it had actually made me any happier and it honestly didn't. And finally swallowing that bitterness left a taste so bad in my mouth that I should've been heading to brush my teeth, but instead I started making phone calls because I was heading somewhere else the second I got home.

3

SLEEPWALKING THROUGH MY LIFE

To my benefit there weren't many PetWorlds in Manhattan so Amber Miller wasn't very hard to find at all after I decided that I needed to speak to her. In fact it took me all of ten minutes before I got the right location and they really needed to be more careful about who they gave out information to because it could have been some crazy man calling for her instead of me.

Living so close to the park and Times Square meant that there was no such thing as light traffic ever and I really wasn't in the mood to sit in the sun barely getting anywhere for an hour so I grabbed Keith's leash and portable water dispenser before we took the two mile walk over to the PetWorld Groomery.

I had already been planning to bring Keith with me to have an excuse to talk to Amber, but I knew I had to make it up to my baby after spending the morning digging out her walker instead of letting her go outside to play. We had never been to this location since I usually took her to the one in East Harlem because they had all services there including the doggy day camp when I knew I would be out late or the dog walker couldn't get her for some reason.

I spotted Amber immediately after coming in even though she was crouched down putting bags of food on a bottom shelf. I recognized her ass though and I licked my lips at the view of her black panties peeking out from the top of her khaki pants. Maybe this wouldn't be so bad after all. Maybe I would even get to see it bare if everything went according to plan. She seemed like the type that might relax once she got some drinks in her, but I shook those thoughts off and unleashed Keith to approach her first to break the ice.

"Hey!" she chuckled out as Keith licked the skin on her elbow as a hello. She immediately sat the last bag down then turned to pet her, but the warm smile she had for my canine friend quickly dropped at the sight of me as she tensed and stood to her feet. She looked around probably trying to see if one of her managers was around before she lit into me again. "Are you trying to get me fired from here too?"

"No. I came to tell you that I know it might seem like it, but I'm not an incel. I can't be. I mean I'm rich and I'm handsome and I have sex whenever I want to. In fact I just had sex with my dog walker before I came here," I informed her, but it didn't seem to move her. Honestly it hadn't moved me much either because I had only done it to prove a point to myself.

"Congratulations. But none of that negates how you see women and handsome is debatable, rich boy," she said before she pet Keith's head once more then tried to leave the aisle, but we were already on her heels. "What do you want?"

"What makes you think I want something from you?"

"Because the only time people with money come sniffing around me is when they want something and something's telling me you're no different."

"Well I don't."

"You're lying. And looks like somebody finally rocked your shit, huh?" she said pointing at the side of my face that Cam had hit the hardest and I was almost amused, but I wouldn't let her know that.

"I bumped into a door the other day."

"Right. I'm sure you deserved it," she said and I finally noticed that she just so happened to also have a healing bruise above her eye.

"Did your man do that to you?" I asked and was disgusted with myself because I was sounding too much like Cam and Chase, but I wasn't trying to be a simp or anything like that. I just couldn't ignore it in case being around her would pull me into a dangerous situation.

"I beat the shit out of my roommate after she touched my stuff, but she got a lucky shot in before the cops came," she said informing me of her ratchetivities, but I didn't particularly care so I cut to the chase.

"Alright so what if I do want something from you? Would it be worth your while if I said I would pay you for it?"

"There's not enough money in the world," she said probably thinking that I was still talking about having sex with me as she continued walking to the end of the aisle.

"It's not like that. And I can double what you were making at Bean," I said which made her pause for a second, but it must not have been enticing enough because she continued on anyway which made me even more desperate.

"Triple it then because I don't want to be alone for the rest of my life and I need to impress my boss this weekend and I stupidly told him that I was seriously dating a woman named Amber and I don't know any other Ambers let alone one who saw through me like you did so I need you to help me get my shit together so I can get a promotion and hopefully get married someday," I said laying everything out for her and hoping that something resonated. I knew that it had when she turned to face me.

"What would I have to do? Because I'm not gonna help you manipulate women who have already wised up on you."

"No, nothing like that. I just want you to teach me how to respect women and help me seem more trustworthy at work." I knew it would've been cheaper to just mimic a nigga like Cam, but I didn't want to go that far. I still had some pride left after all. She just laughed at me.

"What? I'm serious. We can do stuff together and you can tell me everything I'm doing wrong and then I'll fix it."

And even though I didn't actually need to find somebody from her agency just yet, I'd still reached out to a famous but discrete matchmaker because at the end of my break I planned on finding somebody for real. But first I needed to learn how not to fuck it up which was where Amber came in.

"So you want to date me?" she asked with wrinkled brows.

"Well not for real obviously," I said unintentionally scoffing at the idea of wifing somebody like her because I wasn't actually trying to offend the one person who I needed the most right now. She sighed before rolling her eyes and opening the door to the employee part of the store. "Alright sorry. I'll quadruple it."

"You know you could just take that same money and hire somebody to pretend to be Amber for your boss, right? He doesn't know me."

"I could, but like I said if I want to have a family one day I know that I have to work on some of my more questionable personality traits that you may not have been completely wrong about."

"You mean like the fact that you're an incel?" she asked in a tone that told me the conversation would be over if I didn't finally admit it.

"Yeah that and I figured that we already fooled a cop into believing we're a couple so I know we can definitely fool my boss. Then after that I'll use what you teach me to find somebody. Deal?"

"Okay deal," she said as she shook my hand. "But how do I know that you'll actually pay me? If I agree to do this then I need like a nonrefundable deposit or something like that."

"Well how do I know that you won't take that down payment and skip town without even helping me?" She shrugged like that was none of her concern.

"Guess we'll just have to trust each other...after you pay me," she added with no humor but with her hand out.

"I don't trust anybody and it's served me well so far."

"Same, but I'm not the one who needs help so either pay up or shut up, rich boy." I grumbled as I pulled out a hundred dollar bill and gave it to her for her time today. Her broke ass seemed impressed until she spotted the other few hundreds that I always kept in my wallet for emergencies. I kissed my teeth as I handed them to her too then told her to meet me at the Bean across the street from here.

"I can't. I already took my break. Give me your number and we can meet somewhere later."

"No. Quit. Starting now I need your undivided attention for the next month. Did I not mention that part?"

"Yeah pretty conveniently too. Look, I can't just not work for a month. I don't work. I don't eat."

"Well this is your new work and since I know you're not about to give me that cash back anytime soon, you better figure something out and meet me outside in ten minutes," I told her sternly as I put Keith's leash back on and headed for the door.

"Alright, but let's get one thing straight. You may be paying me, but you're not the boss here. I am," she said to my back.

"Yeah yeah. Ten minutes."

Twelve minutes had come and gone and me and Keith were still out front in the sweltering heat looking like loitering tickets waiting to happen. Amber looked pretty sketchy so I figured she could have easily left out of the back and made off with the money, but I hoped that she was doing what she said she would. Just when I was about to use Keith to track her like we were in *The Hound of the Baskervilles* she emerged from the double sliding doors.

"You're free to go?" She nodded. "What did you tell them?"

"I said my grandmother died and I needed time off."

"That's a fucked up thing to say. You couldn't think of anything else?" I asked reflexively because of how close I was to Gram. I had lied about a lot of shit in my life, but I would never include her in them.

"Don't worry. I've been wishing death on her my whole life and she's still alive and kicking. In the end it'll just be her and the cockroaches," she said sarcastically as she walked in front of me to cross the street but stopped so that I would have to open the door for her. I sighed to myself but did it anyway because this was what I was signing up for.

I never understood why not doing simple, supposedly chivalrous acts was such a big deal when it was just because back in the day some old white dudes had decided that men were to do certain arbitrary things to prove that they loved women. I was about to bring this up to Amber when a barista leaving the coffee shop approached me instead.

"You can't bring that dog in here," she said pointing at Keith and I sensed that her sudden hostility was because we were black since everybody knew that white people loved all animals but especially dogs.

"Actually, it's my service dog and please don't ask me about my disability because I will own every Bean on this island when I'm done with my lawsuit against you, the franchise owner, and corporate," I informed her then let the door close behind me in her face.

"I didn't know you had a disability," Amber said sympathetically once we were seated and I'd tied Keith's leash to a chair.

"I don't. I was just giving her the same energy she gave me."

"But still that's a shitty thing to lie about," she said calling me out, but I waved her off.

"So is you killing your grandmother to get out of work. Besides who is this hurting? A blind man couldn't even see it to get offended," I joked.

"Whatever," she said as she approached the register to order a Trenta berry refresher drink and two double chocolate chunk brownies. She then looked back at me expectantly to come pay for it. "You cheap bastard," she said when I didn't move fast enough which garnered a laugh from the cashier.

"I was gonna get it," I lied as I handed over my card because I was sure she didn't spring for an extra-large on her own dime. "But it's not like you can't afford your own shit with as much as I'm about to be paying you."

"Oh no. That's rule number one. My fee doesn't include expenses."

"You know for this to be your first time doing something like this, you sure are adapting to the role easily."

"What can I say? It's that innate Harlem hustler in me. Besides I didn't make the rules. Men did so blame your peoples, not mine," she said as she took a big bite out of the brownie. "Alright tell me what you usually do. How do you meet women?"

"On apps most of the time because I work a lot. I'll start with a coffee date like this to make sure they're comfortable and to see if we have chemistry without the pressure of being 'on' for a first date," I gestured around to show her, but she wasn't impressed by my spiel.

"No, coffee dates are a low investment with a high return and you can't do them anymore. If you're genuinely trying to change then you need to stop thinking like a banker while we're together."

"Well what's wrong with thinking like a banker?"

"Besides being morally bankrupt, there's nothing wrong with it when you're at work. But outside of work you need to stop being an idiot and try hard to think like a woman. It's not exactly rocket science. We just want to be treated like people," she said while finishing the last bite and sucking on the melted chocolate that'd gotten on her thumb. Seeing her thick lips move in that way almost distracted me from my point, but I cleared my throat and got back focused.

"No, you women just want your *brownie* and to eat it too. Y'all spout all of that feminist bullshit, but feminism is supposed to be about equality for everybody, right? So why can't I treat you like I would treat another man?" I asked thinking that I had her cornered, but I was mistaken.

"Because in spite of recent dating trends swinging things even further in your favor, men are still mostly useless. You don't want a wife for love and companionship. You want a porn star that irons your clothes and raises your babies," she said and I couldn't lie and say that the thought of that wasn't pretty tempting. Still I couldn't let her win the argument so I fired back.

"Calm down. This isn't the fifties. I thought Destiny's Child said y'all were all independent women now. What happened to that?" I asked her condescendingly, but she was still yapping away and not listening to me.

"And why should I give up the few perks that I'm entitled to under patriarchy when I don't see you giving up any of yours? Also feminism is about liberation from sex-based violence and oppression FYI. Nobody wants to be treated like a man. Shit look at how y'all treat each other," she remarked as she pointed at my eye and that let me know that she was much smarter than she looked. Or maybe I was just dumber than I looked.

Either way I knew I had bitten off more than I could chew by coming to her for this, but she was still my last hope if I wanted to start being taken seriously and eventually have the life I wanted.

"Let's get this to go."

We walked back across 93rd street to the park and found ourselves an empty bench to settle on like the one we had met on last week, but this one was near a tree so we had some natural relief from the heat.

"Why did you want to leave Bean all of a sudden? Didn't want another one of your *Richie Rich* trust fund kids to hear that you're spending yours on a beard?" she quipped as she sipped on her cool drink.

"You're not my beard because I'm not gay. And I may have some money, but I still grew up in Harlem just like you," I said downplaying how much I was worth because for all I knew she could be setting me up to be robbed by her thug friends. "What about you? What's your story?" I said pretending to be interested because I couldn't care less. I just was tired of her reading into every detail of my life already.

"Well I wasn't born with a silver spoon in my mouth like you so I did what I had to do to get myself out of a fucked up situation, but I'm legit now and I'll work twenty jobs before I ever go back to that street shit. I don't have much, but it's all mine."

"Wait you were a prostitute?" I asked looking over at her because she didn't have that ridden hard and put up wet look that most of them had.

"No nigga! I sold weed. Why is your mind always on sex? And this isn't a movie. You don't just quit something like that."

"How would you know if you really weren't in that life?" I challenged.

"Because I know somebody who tried to but didn't get out of it," she said vaguely before changing the topic back to me. "Okay tell me about your longest relationship?" she asked, but I drew a blank and shrugged. "Your last relationship?" Still nothing. "Have you ever even *had* a relationship?"

"Look I can have any woman that I want," I said not even trying to boast, but she cleared her throat to remind me that it wasn't' true anyway. "Any woman except for you apparently. But that's why I came to you. You could see that incel shit on me from jump so I need you to get it off of me. I know I can have them all temporarily, but I need you to help me get one to actually stick around. You don't seem particularly skilled, but you at least know what you're talking about in this area," I said being a little too candid and I winced because I knew that one would cost me big time. "My bad. I forgot the word for five times, but yeah five times your pay."

"Quintuple," she said after taking a deep breath then turning to me, but I was confused for a second. "You're *quintupling* my pay," she repeated and I was impressed that she knew it off the top of her head when a math whiz like me was stumped. She was full of surprises already.

"Alright let me start with my first assessment of you, Chris. Objectively you're good looking, you're tall and you have money. You should have women begging to be yours, but you don't because you're like Scrooge all year round and that's not sexy especially for the women I'm sure you're going after. Now I highly doubt you went to all that trouble getting your degrees, not developing a personality, and working your way up the banking ladder just for bragging rights.

No, you did it to attract a certain type of woman only now that you can get them you seem to have resentment because they only want your money. This combined with your moderate levels of misogyny is why you fit in the incel category even though technically you're sexually active."

"I knew that already from google. But what's wrong with me wanting to be wanted for who I am and not what I have?"

"There's nothing wrong with that, but you're rich, mean, and stingy. You wouldn't even date you so why would somebody else let alone a beautiful, single woman with options?" she asked and I had never thought about it like that, but it was true. I would never date a woman as jaded as me and I definitely would never date a woman with as many bodies as I had.

"So what then? I should find somebody like you?"

"No, because women like me know better and would only be after your money too. You gotta do the work before it's too late. What are you, thirty-five?"

"I'm twenty-nine."

"Damn you really need to cut back on the coffee and the cigarettes then because your black is cracking just like those white dudes in your office and if you lose that hairline it's over for you," she said laughing at me as I looked at my reflection on Keith's water dispenser. After a minute she took it from me to give some to Keith who had apparently been begging at my feet.

"I'm surprised your dog likes you so much since they're usually great judges of character. Then again he's probably just partial to his own kind," she quipped implying that I was a dog too.

"Actually he's a she. She's just always begging so I named her after the begging-est nigga that there ever was," I said as I scratched behind her ears while she drank. This was the only bitch I loved, I thought, but hopefully with Amber's help it wouldn't stay that way for much longer.

All of a sudden she looked down at her phone then back up at me.

"Chris, I'm not trying to scam you or nothing like that, but I need a little more cash to pick up something important like right now."

"What do you need it for?" I asked then thought to myself that this was why I hated being around poor people. They were always asking for something and they had a different sob story for every day of the week.

"Drugs," she said sarcastically after she'd seen me looking at her arms that I noticed were covered in small, healed puncture wounds now that we were out in the sun. They were too big to be needle marks, but they weren't as noticeable on her dark skin.

"Alright no funny shit. It's for my prescriptions," she finally said when she saw that I expected a serious answer.

"And that cash from earlier isn't enough?" She looked at me like it should have been obvious it wasn't if she was asking before I inquired about how much more she needed. "You're joking. That's a lot of medicine. You got a House In Virginia or something?"

"No stupid. Look my roommate flushed my shit when I was at work last week and Walgreens and Medicaid said it's not their problem since I just refilled everything. That's the only reason I'm sitting here at all talking to you because another few days without my meds and I'm as good as dead, alright?"

"Okay, but you're really not gonna tell me what the medicine is for?"

"Unfortunately it's not for leprosy otherwise I'd definitely have slept with you by now," she said and the thought made me chuckle.

I went with her to pick it up at the nearest pharmacy, but I was still surprised when she ripped off the bottom of her receipt to show me that she wasn't lying about the cost. Once again I was curious about what she may have had, but as long as it wasn't contagious then it wasn't any of my business. What I was concerned with though was where she was going with it when I remembered her mentioning problems with her roommate and something about cops being called.

"Now what's all this nonsense going on with your roommate? I don't need y'all killing each other before I get my money's worth out of you."

"It's not a problem anymore. I left before I caught a case fucking with her trifling ass."

"And where are you staying at now?" I asked before she named one of the seediest hotels in Manhattan. I'm talking hourly room bookings and 'roaches and bedbugs greeting you at the entrance' seedy. I only knew about it because a couple of the guys at work talked about taking women there because it was the last place their wives would ever suspect. "So technically you were homeless when I asked last week then?" I asked and she genuinely smiled at me for the first time.

"I'm not homeless. Just between homes until I can find another roommate, but I probably won't luck up on something until the end of the month."

"You wanna keep looking or you wanna stay with me while we're doing all this?" I offered surprising myself just as much as it did her.

"Yo are you sure you're from Harlem? Because niggas from Harlem don't just ask strangers to come live with them."

"Niggas from Harlem don't do a lot of shit that we're about to do. But like I said I've got some important shit coming up that I need to make a good impression for and you need somewhere safe to stay. It's a win-win because we'll have more time together and of course you would have your own room."

After interrogating me for a minute about who I lived with and what kind of company I kept, she asked to see my place before she agreed as if anything I showed her could be beneath the rock bottom standards that she was accustomed to. But I decided to humor her even though I knew a trap house would be better than where she was currently laying her head at night.

Keith and I were both finally tired of the sun and walking for the day so I tried to hail us a cab for all of two minutes before Amber got frustrated and just did it herself. Not long after a Spanish looking driver pulled in front of us when he thought it was just her, but he tried to pull off when I walked over.

"No dogs," he barked at her while looking at

me and I just laughed at this nigga who was like a shade lighter than me trying to discriminate. I told her not to hold the man up, but she told me to let her handle it.

"Papi. Papi. Be easy. No funny shit. I know it doesn't look like it, but this guy's got money and the faster you get us where we're going, the better he'll take care of you. Got it?" she told him more than she asked as she got in and brought Keith with her. She then looked back at me annoyed that I was holding things up. "What are you waiting for? Get in and tell him the address." And I did.

"That's where you live?" she asked surprised, but before I could answer she was calling him out for putting on his turn signal. "Mm mn. Papi, I see you trying to take Broadway when you know Columbus is quicker," she said playfully before she struck up a good rapport with the man.

You would have thought that they were reunited old friends the way they began complaining about the weather and the tourists he had been picking up. Meanwhile I was just mad that Keith had already pissed a couple times by the pharmacy because I would have loved to see his face when it started to smell in here. Especially since Amber getting along with him proved that she didn't necessarily hate all men off rip so maybe it was just me.

When I opened the door to the penthouse, I realized that the novelty of living here still hadn't completely worn off especially now since I was seeing the place through her eyes. Instantly I could tell she had never been anywhere like this even though she made sure not to show it on her face. I guess she was trying to contain herself because she knew her stay would only be temporary, but all of that went out the door when I opened the curtains and let her get a look at the panoramic view of Central Park which almost made her gasp.

"And that's not even the best part. This place has four terraces. I still haven't even been on three of them yet."

"Why do you need four terraces?" she asked annoyed at the waste of space and I laughed because I had been wondering the same thing the first time I looked at it.

"Hell if I know. It's definitely more square feet out there than it is in here though."

After giving her a quick tour of the sunken living room and the kitchen, I showed her where she would be staying. She looked around for show and inspected a few things, but I knew she was sold when she saw that she had an ensuite bathroom. We were just about to head back out when she suddenly bent and picked up something from the floor.

"What's this?" she asked as she held up a long coral, finger nail. I tried to think of who it could belong to, but I couldn't remember any nails that color being wrapped around my dick in recent memory. I didn't even bother trying to say it was hers after seeing her plain, short nails painted with a clear coat that I just knew she had done herself. "Have this room cleaned before I get back please," she said neutrally, but I took it as a demand which I didn't take kindly even though getting the building's on-call cleaning staff up here wouldn't take more than a quick call to the front desk.

"And just where are you going?"

"To get my shit. Duh."

"You want me to come with you since it'll be dark by the time you get back?"

"Alright, but leave the dog because we don't need two possibly flea-ridden taxi repellants this time," she said looking back at me.

I honored her wishes and called the cleaning service to come by while we were gone. Just like I had imagined the motel room she was staying in was practically synonymous with the word sleazy and I had shoeboxes that were roomier, but then again I did wear a size fourteen.

"This is all you have?" I asked after she'd packed everything up in a few suitcases, a duffel bag and a backpack. She nodded then explained that everything in her old apartment was her roommates and she had just been renting the spare room.

"And I like to think of myself as a minimalist. You know being mindful of my carbon footprint and shit like that," she said unconvincingly.

"That's just the environmentally friendly way to say you're less fortunate, right?"

"Yes and no. But I do prefer to travel light. Always had to," she said simply and even though I was tempted to push for more details I decided not to because I didn't need to know her whole story. I just needed to get out of here because I swore I felt something crawling on me from the second I stepped inside.

We were back to my place in no time and I watched her unpack in less than ten minutes except for the two heaviest suitcases that she just stuck underneath the bed. I nosily inquired about what was in them because I knew if it was clothes, she'd have just put them in the dresser or the closet like she'd done with the other stuff.

"Books."

"Let me see," I told her and surprisingly she obliged without giving me any attitude. Traveling light my ass, I thought because it looked like she was carrying around a lending library with her. I didn't get it. She was wasting the little money she did have on those and I had to let her know that there were better ways to spend it.

"Most of these were thrifted for a couple dollars. I know a place where you can buy them by the pound," she said proudly, but it just proved my point that poor people were resourceful about the wrong shit. I told her that if I was in her shoes I would have been reading get-rich-quick schemes or something financially beneficial not the shit she had.

"Good for you, but I read to escape reality. Not to be reminded that I don't have everything people think I should have. My life may not be like yours, but for the most part it's simple and I like simple."

"Simple is just for people who can't afford extravagant shit. Give me front row on Broadway and Michelin star restaurants or give me death," I joked even though I was serious because there was no other reason to build wealth if I still did commoner shit all the time.

"But what's the point of all that money if you're still not happy? Do you even really like the shit you do or buy or the places you go or are you just into it because it's what you're supposed to be into? Like for example why do you drink so much black coffee when you clearly hate it?"

"How do you know I hate black coffee?"

"Because you grimace every time you take a sip. You don't know how many times I wanted to tell you to just get a fucking latte already," she said and I laughed because I couldn't believe she was all on my body like that without me knowing it.

"Damn I didn't know you were watching me like that."

"Don't flatter yourself. I worked at Bean for two years and I watched every customer that came through the door and you're hard to miss because the only other black men who go to your floor are janitors and they're definitely not wearing those mobster looking suits like yours," she cracked, but I let her get her joke off in peace because I knew my suits were nothing like those guys.

"See something you might be interested in?" she asked hopefully as I thumbed through her collection.

"Nah. These books are old, dirty and germy and I know you don't have good health insurance so remind me to get you a gift card to Barnes & Noble before you leave," I cracked on her back, but she narrowed her eyes at me.

"Yo why are you so fucking socially inept? Like have you ever connected with another human being in your life?" I didn't even bother responding to her question. I just leaned over and took out the long bookmark from the novel on top to let the chips fall where they may. "Look I don't know how they do things where you're from, but where I'm from those are fighting words, my G."

"Please, nobody actually reads where you're from to get mad about a bookmark," I joked then laughed out loud at how worked up she was getting over something so silly as I flipped through another book.

"So it's not just women that you hate then? You also have archaic ideas about low income people. I really can't believe people trust you with money. If only they knew how much of a psychotic nut job you are."

"Are you kidding? That's why they hired me. And how do you know what 'archaic' means?" I ribbed her once more, but she didn't seem to find it funny as she snatched the book from my hands then put it back in the suitcase. I knew she was mad for real when she stopped talking altogether and just went back over to the closet to repack her things.

"Amber! What the fuck?! You've been insulting me all day and calling me stupid idiots and I'm supposed to just take that, but I play with your sensitive ass about books and you're ready to walk out on me?"

"Yeah because I'm doing you a favor here. I don't need this."

"The hell your broke ass don't."

"I may be broke, but even *with* money nobody wants to be around you because your vibe is off. You're like a fox in the chicken coop. Everybody knows there's something wrong with you, but they look the other way because you bring in money. That's why you're not getting promoted. And I bet it's not just women. You don't have any male friends either, do you?" she asked hitting the nail on the head, but all I could think of was some childish rubber glue, back to you shit to say.

"So? You obviously don't have any friends either or else you wouldn't be renting rooms and staying in roach motels. I mean what kind of fucked up person can't even go stay with their grandmother during hard times?" I retorted before seeing that I'd hit a sore spot for real and the hardened expression she'd been wearing since we met looked more wounded now.

"Fuck. I'm sorry! And I'll um…hextuple, no sextuple your pay. Just please go put that shit back and no more arguing until we at least get to what you're here for. And I'm not apologizing for shit else today."

"Well you started it," she accused then mumbled when she walked back into the closet. "And if you keep sticking that big ass foot in your mouth then I'll be as rich as you by the end of the month."

"Yeah yeah. You know you're just like my brother Cam, thinking you're better than people because you read and worship women. You would love his big simpin' ass. He's been trying to save hoes since elementary school. I mean women," I corrected myself after handing her a copy of *Hood Feminism* that had fallen out of her bag.

"Well how is that any different from what you're doing now?" she asked smugly as she took the book then stuffed the suitcases back under the bed.

"It's completely different because what we're doing here is mutually beneficial and I'm giving you money and a place to stay for a service. Technically you're my employee just like my assistant Neal except you're nicer to look at," I reasoned flirtatiously, but she just smirked to herself. "You don't agree?"

"Whatever helps you sleep at night, Chrissy. And touch my bookmark again and I'll kill you and make it look like an accident. I definitely learned how to do that from a book," she said with a smile on her face before an alarm suddenly went off on her phone. "Now is there anything else I can help you with because I'm exhausted and I need a quick nap before we do anything else?" she asked as she yawned then sat down on the freshly made bed.

"I'm beat too, but we should probably get you some keys before it gets too late. Problem is my other set is at the office for Neal. Fuck," I cursed because I knew that he was out of town enjoying his time off from running my life so he wouldn't even be able to bring them to me.

"What's the problem? Just go get them."

"I told you I'm not really supposed to be there this month. Okay how about this? Let's both take a nap then we'll go later on and maybe wear a disguise," I said before I heard how ridiculous it sounded.

"Wait why do I have to go?" she asked like it wasn't obvious that I didn't want her rummaging through my shit or getting any ideas about casing the joint.

"Because I don't trust you here alone yet."

"What, you think I'm a street urchin like Aladdin or something? I'm not getting a trespassing charge for you so I'll just wait outside."

"Nobody is gonna get charged with anything. I just have to make sure nobody sees me because they'll think I'm trying to work and then I'll be forced to take even more time off."

"It's like that on the 42nd floor? I would love a job where they made me take vacations and I damn sure wouldn't be complaining about it like you are."

"Well it's not as fun as it sounds. They're just trying to make me look like I'm not on top of my game anymore when it's really just a sleep activity thing like my doctor said."

"What'd your doctor say about your sleep activity?" she asked nosily and I considered telling her to mind her business like she'd told me about her medicine, but I knew I had to let her know about the naps I was practically prescribed to take throughout the day over the course of my break. But before I could finish explaining everything her eyes had already closed and she was lightly snoring. "Looks like I'm not the only one who needs a few naps," I chuckled to myself as I flicked the lights off on my way out.

A couple hours later when the sun had finally set, I shook my head at her again for refusing to wear all black and sunglasses with me on our quest to get the keys, but she had no interest in pretending that she was in a spy movie with me. I'd made sure that not only did we arrive after the bosses of the bosses were gone since they were the only ones who had any authority over me, but I also had to look out for a few low level snitches who would love to rat me out.

We crept in without being seen by anybody then took the slow service elevator up to the top floor. I hummed the music to *Mission Impossible* to get her in the mood, but she still looked annoyed that I'd dragged her out in the first place and stood as far away from me as she could.

"C'mon at least try to have some fun. Humor me and put these on," I said trying to get her to put on a pair of shades again.

"How about you humor me and tell me what really brought all of this on because I'm starting to get the feeling that it's more than just a promotion and a wife?" she asked curtly which made me frown as I put the glasses back in my pocket. I thought about lying to her but figured telling the truth wouldn't hurt because it wasn't like she knew my family for the information to get back to them anyway.

"My brother's wedding was this past weekend and seeing him so happy with his wife made me jealous that no woman had ever made me feel that way and he had somehow gotten it twice," I said then looked over at her to see her reaction, but she just listened and waited for me to go on. "And then I guess on the flip side I knew that I'd never made a woman feel like that either."

"Do you hate your mother or something?" she asked out of nowhere, but I wasn't taken aback by the question because women had accused me of that for as long as I had been dating.

"I don't even know her," I said lower than I'd meant which made her brows furrow in confusion. "She died having me."

"Oh my god. I am so sorry," she said sincerely as she inched over and closed the space between us.

The hug that she gave me started off stiff and a little awkward, but after a second it felt like it was coming from inside of her. I wasn't even planning on it, but my body led me to wrap my arms around her and squeeze back tightly. I inhaled, expecting to get a whiff of Newports and a metro card but instead she smelled like a soft, feminine scent that I couldn't say I'd ever encountered before.

"Alright that's enough. Get off me," she said before smoothing out her shirt which had slightly lifted when we pushed our bodies together.

I heard a few guys still hard at work when the elevator doors opened, but I led the way as we hustled down to my office at the end of the hall then closed the door as quietly as possible. I found the keys to my place immediately, but the second I grabbed them I heard a couple guys approaching Kemp's office next door to compare conflicting numbers on a live deal so I flicked the lights back off.

They seemed to be going over the entire damn pitchbook right there in the doorway to him so I decided to get comfortable in my chair because I knew we would be here for a while longer. Following my lead, she took a seat across from me and kicked her feet up like she owned the place. I immediately grabbed both of her little feet and placed them right back on the floor because the wood for that desk had costed more than her life. She flipped me the bird then turned her attention to her phone.

"Thanks for that little touching moment back there in the elevator, but I don't want you to go making up any more theories about me because I didn't have a mother. I still had my Gram and my dad and I grew up just like any other kid on my block so no I don't have any mommy issues that I'm aware of."

"If you say so, but if it's not that then it must be…" she began before I cut her off because I knew what she was getting at.

"Must be what? Don't even go there."

"What? I mean I have eyes so I can see it's not small," she said making me smile at the fact that she'd been looking at my dick, but it quickly dropped as she continued, "but you have always given me weak stroke vibes from jump and this pretty much confirms it."

"Trust me. I know what I'm doing in that area and I've never had any complaints."

"Yeah, but even you said they never stick around for long so remind me to get you *Sex For Dummies* when we go to the library," she said with a delighted smirk, but I wasn't amused.

"Think about what you're saying for a minute. Even if my sex was bad, which it's not, how would reading a damn book help me? People like you need to learn that the answers to life's questions are not between those pages so you should get out every now and then for some real experience instead."

"I'm sure the answers aren't between a woman's legs either, but that doesn't keep you from face planting there every chance you get, does it? Or are you one of those incels who think eating pussy is gross too?"

"I don't think it's gross. I just don't do it. I'm saving that for my wife."

"You're playing, right?" she asked incredulously, but I didn't see the big deal when I had ran across plenty of women who didn't like giving head or were so bad at it that I passed altogether. "Well I guess you can keep your money after all then since now I know why you're single, out here demanding head without reciprocating."

"That's not why I'm single. When your dick is as A1 as mine is, you don't need to do all that extra shit," I bragged, but she didn't look like she believed me. "And I don't demand it, but if they choose to I'm not stopping them either. It's not really my favorite thing anyway."

"Really? I'm surprised a misogynist like you wouldn't love to see a woman on her knees."

"Only certain women," I said as I allowed myself to quickly imagine her giving me a Lewinsky job under my desk.

"In your nightmares, rich boy," she said before looking like she was contemplating something. "You got all of your shots, Sparky? I want to see something," she said referring to me as a dog again. I would have gotten offended except I was curious about where she was going with this line of questioning.

I watched her closely as she reached in her cheap little purse and pulled out a small box of white Tic Tacs probably because I'd had an onion bagel and my last cigarette on the way here. I eagerly took one from her because I knew that she was going to kiss me to try to determine how I was in bed. I guess I ate the mint too fast because she gave me another for good measure before she popped one in her own mouth.

"Now this is the only time I'm doing this so you better enjoy it while you can and keep your hands where I can see them," she said like this was the last thing she wanted to do even though it was her idea.

I followed her instructions and put my hands up like I was being frisked, but I leaned down and softly kissed her neck first. I could tell that even though she was caught off guard by it that she liked it because she bit her lip and gave me more access by tilting her head for me. After a minute she used her hands to redirect my mouth to hers and I immediately got aroused at the way she sucked my lips and used her tongue to explore my mouth. Here I was supposed to be showing off my skills, but instead I was following her lead and letting it happen naturally.

Before long my hands had developed a mind of their own and I let them find the small of her back as I took a seat and opened my legs to make room for her. To my surprise she didn't stop the kiss and instead further stepped into it. And right when they were easing down the yellow brick road of her khakis, the door to my office suddenly opened and startled her so bad she jumped a good five feet away from me.

"Oh excuse me. I didn't know anyone was in here," Kemp said as he quickly exited, but I told him it was fine to come back in as I wiped my mouth and rolled my legs under the desk to hide the evidence of what was about to go down before he turned on the lights and interrupted us. "What are you doing here Chris?"

"I lost my keys and the only spare was here. What do you need?"

"Not me, Smith. He wants those old numbers from the Adler file right away. He's on a rampage in there because one of the analysts didn't know to look at your estimates before turning in his."

"Shit Smith is still here?" I asked because that was all I'd been paying attention to. Smith was one of the main guys behind my benching so I hoped he personally felt my missing presence while he tried to replace me with young boys who could never do what I did around here. "If anybody asks, you didn't see me and I didn't see you," I told him as I thumbed through my drawer for a minute before I remembered that Amber was still here. She had been so quiet standing behind me that it was easy to forget.

"Oh this is my uh...my girlfriend Amber. Amber this is Kemp, the guy who I told you makes me look like a champ at racquetball every chance he gets," I said pretty convincingly and they both awkwardly laughed then exchanged phony pleasantries while I found what he was looking for.

"Thanks. You make sure this big guy gets some rest, Amber," he said to her on his way out, but I knew he was confused because I talked to him almost every day and had never mentioned a girlfriend let alone one who had served us coffee for the last couple years.

"Oh I will," she said then listened for his footsteps to fade the further he went down the hall. "You talk mad different around them," she accused me when we were alone again, but still on a mild high from the kiss, I just shrugged because I knew that it was mainly because my accent got heavier around other native New Yorkers like her.

"So what if I tone it down at work some? I play the game to win. You should try it sometimes because I hear the customer is always right," I said ribbing her before we got back in the elevator after Kemp had texted me that the coast was clear. This time she stood closer to me than before and I couldn't help but wonder if it was because of the kiss.

"So how did I do back there?"

"Not bad, but you still tasted like an ashtray. Who jogs but still smokes in this day and age? You're quitting starting now," she demanded.

I started to tell her she was just mad that she couldn't afford the habit, but I kept it to myself since she was right and I had already planned to quit anyway. Plus I wanted to see if we could get her back to feeling like I had just a few minutes ago.

"Okay but forget about that. You believe me about sex now, right?"

"I'll take your word for it since I'll never actually find out for myself."

"See and I thought this was starting to turn

into a hands on, progressive kind of training," I teased her as I stood over her and her body instantly tensed when I invaded her corner. "Hypothetically speaking how much more would I have to pay you for a sample?"

I knew I was pushing it and I knew from the frown lines that suddenly formed on her forehead that I'd ruined the moment, but I couldn't stop myself from inquiring after seeing how much she was into kissing me. Plus I knew there weren't cameras in this elevator like the others and since the cleaning staff had gone home for the night, we wouldn't be interrupted if we were to take a detour to getting back to my place.

"For you?" she asked with an angry smile that I could tell was a setup for the bitter words that soon followed. "A man like you will never make enough money to be able to afford me, Chris. Look this is a waste of time for real. You're forever gonna be just another rich, spoiled creep. Learn to embrace it, get a mail order bride like your banker buddies and call it a day because no normal, sane woman will ever tolerate you. Like, really think about how revolting your personality is when you look like this and you have money!" she almost shouted at me before storming out of the elevator then the building.

"Okay. Okay. I was mostly joking. The most important thing here is that you finally admitted that you're attracted to me too," I said trying to clear the air without apologizing again, but instead she just walked away heading back towards the park. "Alright I'm sorry for the hundredth time today. Wait up!"

She eventually stopped, but I sighed when I realized that it was just to tie the laces on her shoes. I was only a couple feet away from her when I felt the barrel of what felt like a gun in my back. I wasn't sure until I heard a man's voice tell me that he would blow my head off and if I moved. I could've pissed myself right there, but seeing how scared Amber was when she looked up at me made me evaluate the situation quickly and try to think of a way to get us both away unharmed. Well that was until he demanded that I give him my watch.

"Ay bruh you ain't got to do this. There's an ATM right down the street that we can go to."

"Chris what the fuck? You're haggling with the nigga with a gun? Just give it to him!"

"No! This was my dad's favorite watch. He's dead and it's all I have left of him."

"You idiot! You're gonna be with him soon if you don't hand that shit over," she yelled louder as a distraction before she suddenly kicked the guy in the back of the knee. He went down like a house of cards and the gun went flying into the middle of the street.

"Run Chris!" she yelled and we both booked it out of there and didn't stop until we saw a cop car a few blocks away.

"Are you crazy? He had a gun!" I asked her trying not to be so loud, but my heart was still beating fast and my breathing was erratic.

"Yeah and I had a foot and an opening. What's the problem? You still have your watch, don't you?"

"Yeah thanks. Should we go tell that cop what happened?"

"No nigga! I knew you were a snitch," she said and I laughed so hard she looked at me like I was crazy, but it was just because I hadn't done anything that exciting in years.

The danger and the fun of the situation had my adrenaline high and before I knew it I had kissed her again. I must've done something really right because her knees suddenly gave out and I had to catch her before she fell. She was as still as a statue for a minute before she was able to stand on her own again.

"What the hell was that and where are your shoes?"

"Delayed reaction to the gun I guess, and they would've held me back so I lost them," she said as she wiped her mouth. "And don't ever let your lips find themselves anywhere near mine again or I'm gonna bang on you and tie 'em in a knot, you feel me?"

"Yeah I feel you. I also felt you feeling my kissing skills," I teased her as I scooped her up and threw her over my shoulder. The streets weren't too bad over here as far as glass or anything like that, but just in case I carried her until we got to my building.

"Now do you see why I try not to go passed 96th street? I'll stick with the Haves over the Have nots any day," I told her as I hung up my keys and went to pet Keith, but she ran past me right into Amber's waiting arms.

"So you're really scared to be around your own people like that?"

"Yeah because I'm smart. Look what just happened on fucking Park Avenue by one of my people. You might be used to shit like this, but I'm not."

"Nah my life was pretty chill lately until you showed up. All I did was work and sleep then work some more."

"Same. Just with less sleep. That's why my doctor wants me to get as much as possible during this break."

"I doubt that, but we'll make time to sleep in between the whole incel extraction process because I like my naps too," she said as she walked over to her room with Keith not far behind her.

"So you are gonna stay and help me then?" I

asked as I tried to get Keith to come with me to give Amber some privacy, but she shooed me away because she didn't mind having company for the night.

"Yes so go get some sleep because we're getting started early."

"Not too early. This has already been one long, wild ass day with you."

"And just think. It's only the beginning," she said with a curt smile before she closed her door in my grinning face.

I laid in bed that night trying to wrap my mind around how I'd gone from going to ask for her help to somehow ending up living with her and having a near death experience. I sighed thinking of what else could possibly be coming next because like she'd said, this was only the beginning.

4

TROUBLE SLEEPING

I wasn't surprised when I got up that morning to find Chase in my room. I knew he'd been wanting to talk shit about Cam and the wedding, but I had been dodging his calls for the last couple days because I didn't want him to come by and see my face until it'd healed.

"Didn't you just say you were done with female chefs last week?" he asked jumping on my bed like he was five years old to wake me up.

"I am."

"Then why is there a woman with a bad attitude downstairs in the kitchen?" he asked and I was confused until everything from yesterday came back to me.

"Oh that's Amber. She's not a chef. She's my new uh...life coach I guess," I said as I rolled over and ignored his jumping because I wasn't ready to get up yet since running for my life last night had worn me out.

"Life coach?" he asked incredulously before

taking his final jump. "What do you need a life coach for? You're letting a woman tell you how to run your life?"

"Yeah why does that sound so crazy to you?"

"Nigga have you met you? Blink twice if this is some *Misery* shit and you're being held against your will," he joked so I felt the need to downplay the situation since he wouldn't understand what I'd been going through anyway.

"Shut up. I'm not even taking it seriously. It's just something to keep me busy until I can go back to work."

"I feel you. She's cute too if you get passed that mean look on her face," he said and I grinned thinking of what spicy shit she had probably said to him.

"It's not like that. Strictly business with this one," I promised because I saw things going really wrong if I kept trying to get at her in that way and I needed her to be here to fix me.

I finally sat up and planted my feet on the ground and all thoughts of Amber were gone immediately when I took off my sleep mask. Without even saying anything Chase already knew what'd happened.

"Cam did that? Ay we're jumping that nigga next time he's here and he better not deposit my check either," he said being super petty so I chuckled.

"Don't be like that. You seen that girl. You know he needs double that just to feed her. And besides the whole thing was my fault," I said owning up to the fight which seemed to amaze him. "It's still fuck that nigga, but it was my fault. I can admit it."

"Damn she's changing you already. How much does she charge?"

"You don't want to know." I got up to take a piss and grab my robe, but he was still waiting for me at the door when I came back out.

"Did he bring up the house to you?" he asked because finally putting my dad's house on the market was the one thing that he and Cam had agreed on lately. I was the only one still holding out though because the idea of strangers living in our house just didn't sit right with me.

"No and I hope you're not either because I had a long night and I'm not trying to hear that shit right now."

"Why not? Nobody is ever gonna fucking live there again, Chris. Why are we holding onto it?" he asked for the umpteenth time, but I ignored him just like I had done all the others.

"Good morning Amber," I warmly greeted her as I came down the stairs. She spoke back as she whisked something together in a big metal bowl, but she kept her eyes on then narrowed them at Chase. "Y'all good?"

"Yeah, but I thought you said your brother was nice and married."

"No I said he was a simp and that's Cam. This simplet over here is Chase. He wants to be a dog like me, but he can't hang."

"Whatever. I told you my bad for the mix up," he said to her waving off her attitude that no doubt came from him pushing up on her hard before making his way up to my room. He then turned to me and explained his presence here. "Me and Parker got into it and she suggested that I come stay with you for a few days until *she figures out what she wants*, whatever that means," he said before I looked over at Amber.

"You know I don't mind you crashing, but it'll have to be on the couch because Amber has the other room for the next few weeks. Or maybe you could go back to dad's house so somebody could actually be living there?" I asked in a playful higher tone.

"That's real cute nigga. Where are your keys?" he asked and I nodded over to the wall hook by the door. "Alright I'm out then. Unless you two aren't doing life coaching shit all day then I'll stay and kick it."

"We are," Amber said speaking up quickly. Chase laughed then told her it was nice to meet her on his way out, but she just closed the door and locked it behind him. "I don't like him. And I see why you've been through so many chefs since apparently getting sexually harassed by your brother is allowed."

"It's not. He just tries to get the new ones before I can because he hates my sloppy seconds," I told her, but since she looked disgusted at the thought I inquired about what she was cooking since it looked like a hodgepodge of ingredients laid out on the counters.

"This isn't to eat. Your skin is trash and needs some self-care and you need to stop associating negativity with things that you perceive to be feminine so I figured that we could kill two birds with one stone and have a spa day."

"Sounds good, but I'm not putting that shit on my face and the place I go to needs to be booked months in advance," I said reminiscing on the last time I'd been there. Fuck a fairytale. Those were the kind of happy endings I wanted.

"No we're not going anywhere. I already checked your fridge and pantry and you have everything I need right here that'll work even better than the overpriced Swedish mud you're probably used to," she said and I laughed because I did not pay for no damn mud baths, just facials and full-body massages.

"How did you learn about all of this? A book right?" I teased her while watching her throw a few more dried and fresh herbs into the concoction.

"Of course because when you're '*less fortunate*'," she said sarcastically with air quotes, "you have to read and learn all the life hacks."

"I bet, Brokie," I said continuing to tease her until she scooped up a glob of her mixture and smeared it on my face. It was a quick moment of genuine playfulness from her which I welcomed, but she tucked it back in just as fast as it'd popped out and began applying it on me normally.

"I know this might sound random, but looking at Chase made me realize that your family has really good eyebrow genes. I would kill for these."

"Yours are decent. Not sharpies, but not wispy lines either," I said then told her the story about Reese and my fucked up Soulja Boy phase and she thought it was hilarious.

All of a sudden I realized that I was sitting here getting a facial and discussing my good eyebrows with a woman. She was talking to me like I was one of her friends and like I said I wanted to change some but not too much. I had gotten a little too close to the simp edge so I reversed and went back to regular Chris mode. I licked her finger as she applied some near my mouth.

"You know I'll literally kill you, right?" she

casually threatened me and I laughed because I figured her response would be something along those lines.

"I know. It just smelled so good that I wanted a taste. What's in it?"

"Mostly lemon, sugar, and olive oil," she said then told me what everything would do for my skin. I'd detected a hint of honey too and it made me drift off into a quick daydream wondering what she tasted like.

"You ever do stuff like this for your man?" I asked curiously because it seemed like she'd done this before, but she quickly shook her head no.

"Don't have one, but if I did I wouldn't. What does he need his skin all bright and glowing for when I would be the only light he needs in his life?" she quipped and it made me smile. I closed my eyes as she began to really work it in and her soft fingers rubbing on my face was oddly really getting it done for me. "How does that feel?"

"It's making my dick hard to be honest," I told her while reaching down to adjust myself because I didn't feel like I had to lie to her since she already knew I was a piece of shit. It was actually kind of freeing that I could say what was on my mind since I was so used to censoring myself around women until after I got what I wanted from them. Maybe cashing her out wouldn't be so bad after all.

"You'd better think about your grandmother and quick before I cut it off," she said as she nodded towards the sharp knife she'd used to chop the lemon and herbs.

I'd assumed that the soothing facial and a couple hot towels would be the end of her home spa day, but she had something else in her repertoire for me. She claimed that the ginger and citrus bath she'd planned for me would help rid my body of toxins and restore me and I had to look at her again to make sure that this was the same foul-mouthed Harlem girl I'd sought out yesterday.

Broke women must have been evolving without me knowing because if they all had stuff like this up their sleeves, I might've had to reconsider excluding them from my dating pool after all.

"You want to get in there with me so my toxins can mix with your toxins?" I suggested trying to see how far I could push her, directly going against my earlier thoughts about not sleeping with her.

"I don't have any toxins," she said as we made our way upstairs to my room. I pushed the door open for her because her hands were full with a bowl of bath food, but I saw her curiously look around to see how I lived up here.

"You live in New York. You have toxins.

C'mon. Shouldn't you also be teaching me how to be around women in sexual situations but not act on it?" I asked before she reluctantly agreed and told me that it had nothing to do with me. She claimed to just want to feel the jets on her back in the master tub because hers didn't have that feature.

I already knew she wouldn't be down with getting naked so I gave her a pair of swimming trunks and a dark t-shirt to wear after she called me out about trying to give her a white one so I could see her nipples. I wasn't shy about my body though so I stripped down right in front of her before putting on my trunks. Of course she tried and failed not to look.

"Who's Carolyn?" she asked about the tattoo on my chest when I removed my shirt. "Is this the one who broke your heart and made you this way?" she asked smugly trying to hide the fact that as much as she hated to admit it, her eyes had still wanted to see my body in a state of undress.

"It's my mother's name." She instantly looked like she wished she could pull her foot out of her mouth, but I wasn't bothered by it and told her the story of how I'd gotten it. "It was on my eighteenth birthday because my dad and Gram wouldn't let me get it before that. I planned on getting her face too, but I couldn't take the pain."

"That's sweet, but it worked out because this looks like you got it done at Black Ink or something," she said clowning me about the poor quality then laughed harder when I told her that she was right and I'd gotten it at the 125th street location. "I have a tattoo guy that'll fix that for you if you want."

"Nah it's cool," I said as I watched her carefully place my bigger shirt over hers then remove her smaller one so I wouldn't get to see even an inch of skin before she sat down in the water.

Thin slices of orange and ginger and sprigs of rosemary and sage leaves floating in the large tub made it look like a nice little oasis right in the middle of my bathroom. The ginger had turned the water a yellowish brown and it was unusual but appealing and calming in a way I'd never seen. She had ran the water damn near scalding hot though and looked devilishly satisfied when I had to inch in.

We were at opposite ends, but she was still nestled between my open legs and hers naturally rested on top of my thighs. The water just covered her toes, but every time one of us moved I would get a quick glance at how well maintained her feet were. I'd been expecting ugly, calloused feet by the look of the kicks she wore to work, but they were soft and pretty enough to kiss.

I didn't know which ingredient was the culprit or if it was a combination of them all, but something in there was making us sweat a lot after sitting for just a few minutes. She still looked really relaxed though even with the beads of water running from her hairline down her face. It looked like she was dozing off for a minute until she tapped her face then quickly sat up to keep herself awake.

"Didn't get enough sleep last night?"

"I never really do. It's my curse," she said with a wide and contagious yawn. "You feeling toxin free yet?"

"Yeah. Too bad it's also making me smell like Panda Express or I would do it more often." Her eyes were already closed again, but she still smiled at me.

"It does kinda smell like that, doesn't it? Don't worry it'll go away when we rinse off. The important thing is that you're gonna feel and look good enough to eat again when I'm done with you today."

"You think I usually look good enough to eat?"

"You used to back when I first started working at Bean, but any attraction I may have had went away when I saw how rude you were," she said and I kissed my teeth.

"Don't try it. Everybody's mad rude and in a

hurry, but y'all only trip on the customers who don't tip." She laughed and confirmed my suspicion before I remembered that she'd once again admitted she was attracted to me. "And I still think you look good enough to eat too all the time by the way."

"Not even. I saw how you acted when that Kemp dude caught us together last night. Let me guess, I'm cute enough to fuck but not cute enough to be seen with by your work friends, right?"

"Actually I was stunned because I wasn't supposed to be in there at all let alone making out there."

"So it had nothing to do with me?" she asked still in disbelief, but now she had opened her eyes to look directly at me. It was evident that even though she claimed to be some rah rah feminist, just like every other woman out there she still wanted men to find her attractive. I decided to gas her up with the truth to see how far it could get me.

"No. You're a solid six only because of your finances, Amber, but physically I would never rescue anything less than an eight so you're good," I told her as she splashed me, but I could still see the relief on her face.

"And you're a solid two because of your terrible disposition and misogynoir."

"That's misogyny just towards black women, right?" She nodded. "Oh don't worry. I'm an equal opportunity misogynist. I know how hard y'all have it so I would never treat y'all any worse than any other woman."

"Well I've seen the way you treat women so that's not saying much," she said as she reached behind her to add more hot water since it was getting warm.

"Ease up. If I didn't know any better I would think you were trying to cook me in here like that witch in *Hansel and Gretel*."

"You and those bad ass kids would've deserved it," she said to my surprise then sat up again after her eyes had shut again against her will. "What? Look, run up get done up. They were on her property and eating up her house. I would have cooked their little asses too then sprinkled their precious breadcrumbs on top," she said and the mention of breadcrumbs and the delicious scent coming from her boiling us alive was making me hungry.

"Ay you know how to cook?" I asked because she seemed to know her way around the kitchen with all the chopping and preparing she'd done for the facial and bath.

"I'm an adult so yes. You?" she asked and it made me think about Gram and my dad drilling lessons about what it meant to be a man to me.

"Now go on and stir that pot, Christian. I'm not raising shiftless men who don't know how to do for themselves."

"But Gram you already said that we have to pay for everything," I had said at around age ten. "I'm tired of being told to do everything for girls and learn how to cook and do laundry like them too," I'd further complained which prompted my dad to chime in.

"Keep living. Men get tired, but women get tired too. And when a woman gets tired, nothing will get done," he'd advised, but I was the only of my brothers who didn't accept his words as law.

"Not really," I said jumping back to the moment and remembering what Amber had asked me. "And I'm between chefs right now so you should go make us something."

"Only if you do the dishes," she offered and I agreed even though I had no intention on following through.

All of a sudden she said she was getting sleepy again and needed a quick nap first so we got out of the bath then in the shower where she turned the water on ice cold since apparently there was no happy medium for water temperature with her. She had barely dried off before leaving me in there to hang our wet trunks over the shower and get the Colonel's eleven herbs and spices that she'd left behind in the tub.

To my surprise a minute later I found her lying face down on my bed. I had seen her checking it out when she came in and of course I'd thought about getting her in there sooner or later, but I wasn't expecting it to be wrapped in a bath towel and like this. I tried to wake her up for a minute, but she didn't move so I felt her pulse. She was still breathing normally so I just figured she slept hard as I yawned because the relaxing bath had me ready to go back to sleep too.

She was laid across the bottom of my California King, but there was still enough space for me to get in comfortably without disturbing her. Even though we weren't close at all, I still noticed that our breathing had synced as her back rose and fell with my chest. It was hypnotizing and the last thing I remembered before I was also out for the count.

She woke up a little while later in a huff and confused about where she was.

"Relax. You just fell asleep in my bed, Goldilocks," I told her as she gripped her damp towel so that it covered her then stretched and yawned.

"Oh I thought I had made it back to mine. My fault."

"That's alright. I knew I would get you in here sooner or later."

She flipped me the bird then left without

saying another word. I waited for a while for her to ask me what I wanted to eat, but her rude ass had already decided on pancakes and sausage by the time I smelled everything was done. It looked delicious though so I didn't complain as she sat our plates at the counter.

While we ate she told me next up on our Incel Itinerary was visiting the Grand Central Library to get some books on black feminism. I hadn't been there since I was a kid because Gram stressed reading back then and said that television would rot our brains. She let up when we got to high school, but we still had to read at least one book a week because she would expect a thorough conversation about it over Sunday dinner.

I thanked Amber for cooking even though my scraping of the plate had said it all then got up to head to my room to get dressed for the library, but she stopped me in my tracks.

"Aren't you forgetting something? The dishes?" she added when I didn't catch on immediately.

"Oh I'll just get the building cleaning service to take care of them while we're out," I said then went over to the stairs, but she beat me there and sat so I couldn't pass her.

"My grandmother didn't teach me much, but she taught me not to go to bed or leave the house with a dirty kitchen."

"Good thing we're not at her house then. My house, my rules," I said pulling rank, but she didn't budge an inch so I begrudgingly went and washed them poorly on purpose just so she would have to do them over herself, but instead she made me wash them again but better this time around.

"You're in charge of hundreds of millions of dollars a year, but a dish rag and Dawn is where you're stumped? I'm not buying it. Bust those suds, B."

I couldn't do anything but go along with it because her holding me accountable for the things that I promised was what she was here for.

I had officially stepped into her world when we made it to the library. We practically went up and down every shelf looking for apparent words of wisdom that would change me. I wasn't as enthusiastic as she was though especially when I saw a couple bad librarians there that caught my attention because they certainly didn't look like that the last time I was here. But Amber made me stay focused and got us a quiet table in a mostly empty section then put me to work like I was studying for finals or something.

To both of our surprise we actually had a pretty decent and lengthy discussion about the things we were reading. At first it took me a minute to let my defenses down and not get offended by the phrases like male pattern violence and the alleged pornification of society but especially women as a class, but there was nothing to argue about because everything those scholarly women were saying were straight facts. Niggas really weren't shit and we never had been at any point in history.

Amber thought that my unchallenged agreeance with her stance seemed too easy though and she accused me of just going along to get along until we talked about some real world scenarios that I would probably encounter to test how serious I was about applying the things I'd learned today. I guess my responses were acceptable enough because she let me know that this was just the beginning and we would definitely be back, but for now she was done being my Incel Instructor for the day. I chuckled then took a call from the matchmaker I'd been waiting to hear from for the past few days.

Amber shamelessly earhustled on my conversation then lit into me saying that she couldn't believe that there was an actual online catalog of women to flip through then pointed out how it went against literally everything we had just gone over today like seeing women as objects. Still she was curious and wanted to see it though…for educational purposes she claimed.

"Damn. They're all so…perfect," she said and instead of the envy I was expecting to see all I detected was a little self-doubt.

"That's the point. If you want we can shine you up and get you in here too once we're done fixing me," I joked, but she immediately shook her head no.

"Every woman wants a rich man, but it's never that serious. If I can't meet him reaching for the same book in here then it's just not meant to be."

"Well what do you even want a rich man for in the first place? I thought you were all about the simple life also known as boring and broke?" I mocked her and she rolled her eyes.

"I do want the simple shit, but men won't even give you that without complaining so I *simply* raised my prices. Besides y'all are way too aggy to put up with for free," she said and it reminded me of something my dad used to say.

"The only thing a woman should reach inside of her purse for is her lipstick."

"No just admit you're a bird like every other girl in Harlem. It's nothing to be ashamed of. You're in good company because y'all are like eagles compared to those pigeons in the Bronx."

"Whatever. I'll proudly be a pterodactyl for the right check."

"Guess I had you pegged wrong. I didn't

take you for the type that could be bought," I said, but she just shrugged.

"Call it what you want. I prefer my peace and sanity and if I have to compromise on those, which a man will eventually have me doing, then it needs to be benefiting me financially," she said and I was sure I had the perfect response until she went on.

"When you come across a deal at work, do you jump on it right away because it seems good or do you research and run the numbers to make sure it'll be beneficial now and in the long run?" she asked before a short, rhetorical pause. "Exactly so stop trying to shame women into poverty especially when a nigga like you has it like that. I can't wait to meet the woman that's gonna run your pockets. You're not even gonna see it coming," she laughed out.

"That'll never be me. That's what ironclad prenups are for. In fact, I already have one drafted."

"Ooh can I see? I bet there's a no weight gain clause in there, right?"

"You think I'm that vain?"

"Uh yeah. That's why I could never be with a man like you. I at least want a rich guy who I can stand to be around so I can try for a happy marriage. Feminist or not, hetero women got a bad deal being paired with y'all. The least you can do is pay like you weigh."

"Well sorry to be the bearer of bad news, but rich or poor, there's no such thing as a happy marriage."

"So why are you trying to get in one so fast all of a sudden then? And don't just say work because after seeing your office, you're doing better than most niggas your age by far."

"It really is just about work. In order to get to the next level, I need to be complete on paper which means a wife and kids."

"God you really are an incel."

"How does *that* make me an incel? Of course I'll love them and shit, but if it was up to me I wouldn't even be thinking about this for another decade. I just want to sow the rest of my wild oats in peace until my hair starts to thin," I joked even though I meant it.

"Then what's the point of marrying at all then when you're just gonna cheat anyway?"

"Who says I'll cheat?" I asked and she gave me a disbelieving look. "Alright so what if I do? It's not the end of the world. She'll get over it."

"Niggas like you kill me. You won't cheat on your barber, but your wife will just have to accept it from time to time?"

"That's different."

"No it's the same and it just goes to show that you respect your lining more than your life partner which says more about you than it does her. You're not loyal."

"Loyalty is overrated anyway."

"It's not, but that's why I just want to squeeze one Chanel bag out of a dude with money then we can get the whole thing annulled because I can't stand to be around men like you for too long."

"You know how much those things cost? Please tell me that's not what you're gonna use my money for?"

"I don't think it's any of *your* business what I plan on using *my* money for," she said matter-of-factly and raising her voice above the acceptable library whisper we'd been using so far.

"It is because it's a waste. See you women are always buying dumb shit that depreciates. I thought you were at least different in that regard," I ranted then thought about how irresponsible it was considering how little she was paid before me. "What, you make like fifteen an hour? Why don't you just work more and save up to get it?"

"It's complicated, but I can't really do crazy hours like that right now."

"Complicated? Right. Just admit you want Chanel, but you're too lazy to actually pay for it yourself."

"First of all, don't ever call me lazy when

you literally pay somebody to do everything but wipe your ass, rich boy," she began before looking at me like I disgusted her. "Second I didn't say I would use the money I'm earning from this to buy that. Just that I want it someday. And third, don't give me a hard time about one little bag when you still haven't even been on three terraces in the overpriced place that you call a home." She had said a mouthful so I let it sink in before I thought of another comeback.

"I guess I just don't understand why you even want it. What, you gonna wear it to the flea market?"

"No stupid. I don't want to wear it. I just want to have it, but I wouldn't expect you to understand because it's a sentimental thing and you have to have feelings for that."

"I have feelings. But why would you buy something you don't even want to use? At least I actually get some use out of my shit."

"I want it because my mother had a lot of them and she loved them so much that she named me Amber Chanel. She used to tell me how she would give them all to me when I was old enough to take care of them, but when she died my grandmother sold all of her shit," she explained and I immediately felt bad when I looked down at my wrist and saw the watch that I'd nearly gotten us killed over last night.

It was far from the most expensive piece of jewelry that I owned, but it was timeless and vintage and it was my dad's so I guess I did understand where she was coming from and I apologized once again for making assumptions about her. We left the library on a neutral note at closing time and I didn't even slip one of those librarians my number out of respect for Amber because these were her people and for the first time in probably forever, I didn't want to disturb something that meant something to somebody else even if I didn't understand it myself. Chase was right. Her words were actually starting to sink in for me.

♛

For the past few days I had been thinking of a polite way to tell Amber to take down her braids for the party at Reisman's house. I knew I should have said something sooner than the night before, but we had been getting along a little better so I didn't want to mess it up because I knew how sensitive black girls could be about their hair. As expected she stomped around and complained when I brought it up because she hadn't worn them that long.

"Look they're nice or whatever but not the message we're trying to send. I need you to look like those girls in the catalog tomorrow, not *Moesha*."

"Haha. Alright I'll take them down, but since you're the one with the problem then you can help me and pay for them to be done again."

"Whatever. What aren't I paying for at this point?" I asked letting her know that she wasn't actually punishing me especially since I had oddly been enjoying spending time with her lately.

All we did was argue over dumb shit I'd said before I eventually apologized then tried to see things her way, but it was cool just to have somebody here with me. I had never considered myself the lonely type until meeting somebody that was just as alone as I was.

Since we had been talking and I'd observed her more I realized that she really didn't have any friends outside of the people she worked with and even that wasn't anything to write home about. She claimed that she didn't have time for friends, but I knew that it was also because she didn't trust anybody and knowing that oddly made me trust her more because it perfectly described how I felt about people.

I had mistakenly thought that this braid takedown thing could somehow be an enjoyable experience, especially after she got her hair stuff and sat between my legs, but she decided to really make it a torturous task when she set up a

YouTube playlist of feminist videos on the TV in the living room. We had already highlighted the hell out of a few books by bell hooks and Patricia Bell-Scott since she'd been here so I thought that I would get a break for a little while, but apparently that was too much to ask for.

A few videos in Tillar's friend Nicole came on the screen and it surprised me. Everybody knew she did the comic book character costumes and stuff online, but I didn't know that she was into this 'I am woman, Hear me roar' type of shit too.

"You watch Nicole?"

"Every week. I'm obsessed with her," Amber said before looking up at me. "How do you know her?"

"She's best friends with Cam's wife and Chase slept with her once."

"Good for him," she said sarcastically. "But he's probably lying. She's too smart to go for a man like him."

"Nah. Smart girls are always the biggest hoes. Don't let those SAT words fool you," I said before she jabbed me near my nuts with the metal point of a comb. "My bad, I forgot. No more Bs and Hs, I swear."

By the time we were halfway done, I could tell she was getting tired so I finally convinced her to let me put on an old Eddie Murphy stand-up special. But instead of laughing at some of my favorite jokes of all time, she had me cracking up harder than he did at the way she kept commenting on how hot he looked in all that red leather under the lights.

Her head jerked hard as she almost dosed off a few times, but we managed to get them all down in no time. I'd surprised myself with how quickly I'd picked up the skill since she'd only demonstrated it to me once.

"Who knew I had a knack for something as random as this?" I asked as I played in her big stretched out, floppy afro. She didn't even stop me and instead rested her tired head on my bare knee. "You didn't sleep again last night?"

"Not much. I kept waking up."

"You think it's because you're still getting used to the bed or the side effects of your medicine?" I asked about the two excuses she'd been using for why she was always so tired.

"Could be," she said before letting out a loud ignorant ass fart. I hit her with a couch pillow then pinched my nose as she laughed.

"Ay you're getting mad comfortable around me and I really don't like that shit. Please stop it," I begged her because living with a woman for the first time already had me seeing a lot of shit that I didn't want to see the past few days. She just smiled up at me.

"I'm trying to repel you, but nothing's working."

"Well you're gonna have to do better than a little gas then because I can hold my breath for a couple minutes," I informed her before I dusted a few dandruff and scalp flakes off of her and myself onto the floor. "And lowkey this is disgusting as fuck."

"It's really not, but that's how I know all my training will be in vain and you'll still end up with a white girl anyway," she said amusedly and I laughed.

"You saw what section I turned to in that catalog. I'm all about black love these days," I said honestly because I had already fooled around and sampled every type in the metropolitan area and even some homegrown European and Asian women when I traveled, but I knew that the only woman I could see myself settling down and having a family with was a black woman.

I didn't want to come home and have to keep up the same mask that I wore at work, careful not to say anything to make myself come off as a stereotype. I just wanted to be able to relax and watch some ignorant shit on TV after dinner without being judged. A night kind of like the one I was having tonight except not with Amber of course. I pictured a young Angela Bassett or Phylicia Rashad type, the women that I had grown up seeing and loving. They were sexy and accomplished but knew how to act in public too.

"You're all about black love these days, you say? Let me guess. Some popular black girl ignored you in middle school and for a while you wanted to get revenge on the rest of us. Am I right?" she asked as she turned to stand and used my open legs as leverage, but before she got up she stopped and looked up at me with a curious look. If I didn't know any better I would swear she was about to give me a blow job from this position, but like I said I knew better.

"Yeah that's actually exactly what happened. How did you know?"

"Because all incels have the same tired story. But riddle me this. Why didn't you ever go for the lowkey girl that was in your league back then?" she asked matter-of-factly, but I put my head down at the uncomfortable thought. She put both hands on my face and lifted it as she repeated herself. I still didn't want to share the reason with her, but I knew I couldn't get out of it with her looking at me the way she was.

"Because even the girls in my league preferred my brothers over me," I told her sounding more vulnerable than I meant to so I cleared my throat and lowered her hands.

Thankfully she changed the subject to herself as she stood then took a seat next to me because admitting that I felt inferior to Cam and Chase back then had a lot to do with how competitive I was today whether I acknowledged it regularly or not.

"Well I wasn't exactly popular either, but I was still popping because I was cool with everybody and their mama."

"Oh I know that type. A little hot ass like you was definitely being passed around by the basketball team," I accused her, but before she could hit me I'd already gotten up and hit the stairs.

"You really going to bed already?" she asked with another yawn like she wasn't half-way asleep already.

"Yeah I've got church in the morning and when I get back we're going to Reisman's thing."

"Don't lie. You do not go to church."

"Yes I do. I take my Gram every Sunday."

"Chris, you really take your grandmother to church? I think that's the most wholesome thing about you. Aww."

"Yeah well my dad used to so I stepped up after he passed. You want to come with us?" I asked even though I knew Gram would have a million questions for me after if I brought her along.

"I'm not much of a church girl. Me and patriarchal religions don't exactly mix well."

"I know. I read about it with you," I said playfully then walked back towards her when I thought of something I'd wanted clarity on. "So you don't think God is real?" I asked because she was much smarter than me about stuff like this so I was hoping she had the answers to the questions I had been afraid to ask my whole life.

"I doubt it, but if he or she is real then they have a lot of explaining to do before I ever step foot inside of a church again," she lamented and I nodded in understanding before heading to bed.

In the middle of a dream of me going balls deep in a Kerry Washington lookalike, there was a light tapping on my bedroom door. I knew it was Amber so I ignored it for a second hoping that she would go away and I could get back to Kerry, but instead she came in and sat at the end of my bed.

"Chris, are you up?" she whispered.

"No," I said purposely being rude until I realized that it wouldn't actually make her go anywhere. "What do you need?" I sat up in bed and rubbed the sleep from my eyes because I knew whatever it was would be more than a minute or two.

"I've got a problem. There's something stuck...inside of me," she said slowly.

"Something?" I asked as I threw the covers back and turned on my light because my interest had been piqued. "Something like what? A vibrator?"

"No idiot! A tampon," she said through tight lips like I was the one who had come to her room and woken her up. I wiped my eyes again to buy time because I couldn't figure out what exactly she wanted *me* to do about that.

"Okay obviously I'm not an expert on those things, but aren't there strings attached for this very reason?"

"Yes, but it must've gone up there too. Look I just need you to get it out, but please don't look at it or me, alright?" she asked as if I had already agreed to it, but who was I fooling? Of course I was gonna do it.

"I won't. Trust me, this is not how I pictured seeing you naked for the first time either," I joked as I got out of bed, but she sighed with a deep annoyance.

"You're not gonna see anything because your eyes will be glued shut. You know what? Forget it. I'll just go to the emergency room."

"No. I'll do it and I won't look. I promise. This is as close as I'm ever gonna get to playing in your pussy so I'll take it," I said lightheartedly, but she was so embarrassed that I saw her dark brown cheeks nearly flush. "Alright. This'll be just another embarrassing thing that we take to the grave like the facial and me doing your braids. Deal?" I asked as I extended my hand which she took her time accepting.

"Deal."

"Okay let's get ready to spread 'em then," I said before giving her a friendly slap on the butt and she groaned at what she had gotten herself into.

A couple minutes later, I found myself still blindfolded by my sleep mask in Amber's bathroom as I tried to initiate the search for what had gone missing, but she was so tense that it was hard to get in. All of a sudden I remembered how relaxed she'd gotten when I kissed her neck before in my office so I did that.

"What are you doing?"

"Trust me this'll help you relax. I'm an expert at period sex."

"But why? You are so damn gross!"

"I thought you were the Head Feminist in Charge so what's the problem with a little blood? It just smells like pennies. Not my favorite type of money, but it's still money," I said playfully and she finally laughed and unclenched her muscles enough to let me in.

It took a little while because it was really up there, but I could sense how relieved she was when she felt me coaxing it down with my fingers. Even when I was done and she was fully covered, she still wouldn't let me remove the mask so she helped me scrub my hands clean then sent me on my way after thanking me.

"Anytime," I said with a wink but noticed that she looked uneasy only it didn't seem to have to do with the tampon issue.

"Are you really going back to sleep?"

"That's the plan. You?"

"I wasn't really sleeping. If I get the least bit nervous, I stay up all night and I'm really worried about saying the wrong thing to somebody important tomorrow."

"Don't worry. You'll find out that outside of numbers, most of those guys couldn't think their way out of a box and don't get me started on their wives. You're gonna do great."

"Thanks, but do you think you could stay and talk for a few more minutes? The sound of your voice really knocks me out for some reason."

"I really bore you that much?" I asked and she nodded.

She wasn't lying either because barely a couple minutes into the forced conversation, her head had already lulled against her pillow which then allowed me to sneak out like a thief in the night.

Amber must have been really thankful for the vaginal excavation that I'd performed on her because when I got up that morning her and Keith were already in the kitchen preparing a feast for me and she didn't even make me wash the dishes after.

She looked different but in a good way with her natural hair out and all over her head, I noted as we had pleasant small talk that didn't involve any incel talk for once. I knew there had to be a catch to all of this though and I was presented with it when I was on my way out the door for church and she had her hand out.

"It's for my hair and makeup and I need a nice dress," she told me with emphasis on nice.

"How nice are we talking?"

"*Nice.* You want me to act like money, then I gotta look like money too," she reasoned before seeing my face and sighing. "Fine. Be a cheapskate and I'll just wear the dress I picked out for my grandmother's funeral."

I knew she was being serious, but I wasn't touching that topic with a ten foot pole so I just reached in my wallet for a credit card.

"Try not to go crazy. No shopping montages on me, alright?" I said because I imagined her acting like she was in BMF and buying up everything from one of the few luxury stores that were open on Sundays.

"Alright," she promised before taking it from my hand then immediately beating me to the door. "Sucker!" she yelled as she ran out and I knew for sure that she would renege so I just smiled to myself and hoped it would be worth it.

I had been to church and back then taken a long, restoring nap by the time I heard Amber coming in later that afternoon, but I was on my way to the shower so I didn't bother going to see what she'd brought in.

I'd reminded her of the time we were supposed to be leaving twice by text while she was out, but I still found myself outside her door knocking so that she would hurry up.

"C'mon Amber. We're probably gonna be the only black people there so we can't be late. Let's go. I'm sure you look fine," I begged her before she told me that she would be done by the time I pulled the car around.

She wasn't. And just when I was about to get out and go personally throw her over my shoulder to get us there on time, she came waltzing out of my building looking like she owned the place.

I guess she was going for a kind of retro look because she had soft and tousled Jessica Rabbit hair and she wore an off the shoulder, pastel pink, tea length dress. And the closer she got I saw that she was even wearing makeup that enhanced the already good features of her face.

I smiled at her new high heeled strut that was extra slow because she obviously couldn't walk in them, but it didn't even matter because she looked good. Her toughness had all but disappeared and she looked nothing like the ruffian with the fat ass I'd found in the park last week. She could pass for a lady.

"You picked that out yourself?" I asked as I opened the passenger door then helped her get in.

"Yeah not bad for a street urchin, right? This is just proof that nobody is actually ugly. We're just broke."

"Nah you're cute in your other clothes too," I complimented her, but I didn't realize that I was still hovering over her so I quickly went back around to the driver's side.

"Aw you think regular Amber is cute, Chris. Maybe you do have a little Prince Charming in you after all," she said sarcastically.

"No. I mean yeah obviously. I wouldn't have saved you otherwise," I said trying to act callous.

I had just been bitching about running into traffic on the drive to Connecticut, but I actually didn't mind it too much because every time we stopped I got to look over at her and enjoy the small talk we were having. She noticed it and couldn't hide the wide smile she had even as she called me out.

"Stop looking over here at me before you crash. I don't want to die before I get to spend more of your money."

"I'm not looking at you. I'm checking the mirror on your side," I said telling one of the most unbelievable lies of my life.

"No you weren't. Look I've read every fake dating book there is, especially the ones with the rich guy, poor girl trope. This is the definitive point in the story where you start falling in love with me so can we just skip all the goofy shit and have you propose now so I can turn you down?" she suggested. I looked over and decided to humor her because she really did look that good.

"Marry me?"

"Never," she said mildly laughing.

I didn't know why it surprised me that she took my hand when we got to Reisman's, but it did. Luckily it wasn't too hot outside, but I still felt my pits and palms getting moist from the nervousness coming from both her and me so I led us over to get a flute of wine from a server. She declined it because she was too anxious to drink so I took the one I'd gotten for her too.

I spotted Kemp and Lewis sitting at further back tables with their wives and kids and figured that we wouldn't be seated too far from them, but Amber peeped our name place settings at the table next to the main one where the birthday girl and the family would sit. And next to ours was another big boss Finestein and his family so we really did have some of the best seats in the yard.

"See just mentioning you have a girlfriend is already getting you perks," she bragged then dusted imaginary dirt off her shoulder as I pulled out her chair.

"Nah I'm not buying it. They're just trying to get the negroes in all of the pictures," I whispered to her as Reisman suddenly appeared by my side to personally greet us.

"Is this the exquisite young lady that you've been keeping a secret from me, Christian?"

"Yes sir. This is Amber Miller. Amber, this is the big guy upstairs Jacob Reisman."

"Mazel tov," she said to him as she took his extended hand and he looked impressed.

"I always knew it'd be a pleasure to meet the woman capable of taming this kid, but I had no idea that Christian was getting more than his morning coffee from you," he said letting her know that he'd indeed recognized her. I didn't know how since he never got his own coffee, but the guy did have eyes and ears all over the building.

"Yes. Unfortunately I gave him a complimentary muffin once and now I just can't seem to get rid of him," she lied and got a hearty laugh from him because no matter how much money we both had, we still had a deep love for free shit.

The ceremony was supposed to have begun already, but apparently there had been a mishap with one of the birthday girl's dresses so everyone was keeping themselves entertained. Amber and I, however, were being treated like guests of honor by Reisman and his wife Jules.

A decent sized crowd had formed around our table because Reisman had begun telling some of his most famously funny stories to Amber because she was probably the only one here that hadn't heard them a million times. I knew what this was because he had done it to all the promising interns and first year analysts at company functions and it was a good sign because he only did it when he really liked somebody.

All of a sudden I felt somebody approach me from behind and put their hands on my shoulder. It was Lewis and I could tell from the forced smile that didn't reach his eyes that he was jealous of all the facetime I was getting with not only Reisman but Finestein as well.

"So Kemp tells me you're a PetWorld employee," Lewis said to Amber out of nowhere. Both of us were unprepared for the sudden outing, but she handled it like a professional before anyone had time to react to the fact that despite her polished appearance, she wasn't actually one of them.

"Yes I'm there part-time on weekends. And just between you and me, I consider it quite the undiscovered life hack that allows me to work with animals while also skipping out on a hefty vet school tab," she said which garnered genuine and phony laughs alike from the crowd.

"That's so endearing. And how do you juggle this passion for animals with your job at Bean? That is you that always remembers to hold my foam, right?" Lewis asked even though he already knew the answer.

"That was me, but no more juggling because as of last week, I'm no longer a part of the Bean family. However, since you were always one of my favorite customers, I'll remind my old coworkers to continue to take care of you," she said sweetly and proving that she could control herself when needed because I'd expected her to give him the same mouth she'd been giving me from the moment we met.

I could tell that her cool demeanor and wit had officially won over Reisman and his wife when they offered to give us and a few others a tour of the house before the ceremony finally began shortly. Reisman went on and on to Amber about how he'd been trying to get me to move out of the city and settle down then he hinted at her pushing me to as well.

After that I gave her the go to let loose and be herself because she could handle it. She had colorful critiques of every subject brought up and she had even researched the ceremony and knew how to participate once it started.

We had only planned on staying for the ceremony and a few minutes of the real party since it was still for a teen girl, but by the time the sun was setting we were having so much fun that we decided to stay longer even though we were both getting a little sleepy. I watched her covertly pull a flask from her purse so I offered to get her something from the bar, but after telling me that it was an energy drink I took a swig too.

It didn't work because we were among the last guests there as the catering staff cleaned up around us because she had fallen fast asleep on my shoulder and couldn't be woken up. I waited around for a few more minutes before thinking what would Cam do? Of course his back probably wasn't equipped to pull off carrying his wife, but I decided to carry Amber back to the car. On the way out I ran into an amused and more than tipsy Reisman.

"Looks like Jules can still throw a killer party," he said looking down at a soundly asleep Amber. "Christian, I just want you to know that I'm really proud of you and what I saw here today. Keep this up and we'll be removing the *junior* from Junior VP sooner than you know it, son," he said sincerely before telling me goodnight.

It was weird because I felt myself getting emotional all of a sudden not just at his praise but also the fact that a man I looked up to had referred to me as son. I wasn't sure that I had made my own dad very proud during his last years on earth so it meant a lot to get it from Reisman.

I got Amber out to the car with no problem, but I accidentally banged her head trying to put her inside because this looked so much easier in movies than it actually was in real life. But even still she remained out cold and it wasn't until we were halfway back to the city that she finally stirred awake.

"Where are we? And what the fuck happened to my head?" she asked crankily as she sat up from her slouched position.

"We're almost home and I bumped it putting you in here. My bad, but you really need to go to bed earlier or something because this shit is getting dangerous."

"Thanks dad," she said dismissively and for some reason it made me angry because she wasn't taking her safety seriously. If this would've happened anywhere else and I wasn't with her she could've been taken advantage of or even worse.

"Well if you actually know who he is you should call him to come talk some sense into your dumb ass before you get yourself killed," I retorted and I knew I had hurt her feelings because she didn't even respond. She just leaned her head against the window and closed her eyes again.

"Sorry, but you need to talk to your doctor about changing your medicine because this is getting out of hand. You're always tired and falling asleep at the wrong time," I said with more concern this time, but she still yawned like there was no importance or urgency to what I was saying.

"Please don't pretend like you actually care about my well-being, Chris. I'm fine."

"You're not fine and I do care. I'm not some robot like you think I am."

"So? I still don't trust you."

"Does it look like I care? I don't even trust me half the time," I said seriously. "I should stop complaining though because you passing out isn't that bad since you're actually quiet for a change," I ribbed her and she smiled.

"Did your boss say anything about me?"

"Yeah, everybody loved you, but more importantly I was standing next to you so they loved me even more. Mission accomplished," I said before holding up my fist for her to dap.

"Glad I could help," she said before leaning on my shoulder again. "My head still hurts. Carry me upstairs when we get back?"

"Never," I told her in the same tone she'd used to reject my fake proposal and she grinned that cute, girlish smile that had been growing on me more than I'd ever admit to her or anybody else.

5

HATE SLEEPING ALONE

Now that we had successfully gotten the Reisman situation out of the way, Amber and I finally relaxed some and took it easy for the next few days. We slept in late, ate breakfast at lunch time, and then took Keith on long walks through the park before heading back to the library.

From spending the previous week with her, I knew that she wasn't on actual drugs anymore, but I still wanted to know about all of these side effects that she blamed on her medication. She was on the strictest sleep schedule I'd ever seen complete with nap alarms that went off throughout the day. At first I didn't think much of it and I had actually been scheduling mine right along with hers, but a few more instances of her falling asleep mid conversation had piqued my curiosity about her medication again.

I finally got bold enough to see for myself one night after looking up medicine that made people sleepy which had gotten me nowhere because drowsiness was a side effect of practically everything. I waited about an hour after hearing her final alarm before slowly opening the door to her room. Keith nearly fucked up everything by barking at me like I wasn't the nigga who had fed her for her whole life, but she laid back next to Amber in bed as I looked through her drawers and bags but came up empty.

But going through her backpack, I did stumble upon a few box cutters, lots of pepper spray and every little key gadget thingamajig known to man that was supposed to protect women from potential attackers. All in all she had enough weaponry in there to take down a giant so I would have been blinded then sliced to ribbons if she had thought to catch me after work one late night for getting her fired.

I knew she must have really been feeling at home here when I finally got the bright idea to check her bathroom and saw that she had stocked the medicine cabinet with what I had been looking for along with other feminine hygiene stuff. I officially felt like I was violating her privacy now, but I justified it because I felt like I had a right to know what had been brought under my roof.

She was out cold, but I didn't want to take a chance on her waking up because she did that sometimes after going to bed so I took pictures of all the unfamiliar medicine names before creeping back out then heading up to my room to google them. I was expecting some weird rare disease or disorder, but the most common results were for narcolepsy and something called cataplexy which was a sudden, brief loss of voluntary muscle tone triggered by strong emotions like laughter.

I was instantly relieved to see that she wasn't going to die anytime soon because I had seen that stuff portrayed in one of those old Rob Schneider movies and aside from not being able to drive, it didn't seem like the worst condition to have. Well that was what I'd thought until google led me to an organization called Project Sleep which had a lot of depressing information on both conditions.

The more I researched the more hopeless I got because over and over I saw that there was no cure. At some point I even reached over and grabbed my wallet to make a donation because although not many people had it, they really did need to come up with something better to help those afflicted with it. I had almost put the donation in Amber's name, but I didn't want her to know that I knew so I didn't. I could have written it in the sky though because the moment I hit submit on the payment page, I heard her voice behind me and she didn't sound happy about what she'd seen me looking at.

"You went through my shit, Chris?" she asked daring me to lie as she held up a small bottle of pepper spray that must've fallen out of her backpack when I was searching it for clues.

"Maybe. What's it to you?" I said coolly like I wasn't seated in front of an angry and potentially unhinged woman who would probably love nothing more than for me to give her a reason to mace me. "Why didn't you tell me about your narcolepsy and that other thing you have?" I asked already forgetting the name.

"Because it's none of your fucking business!" she shouted at me before throwing the bottle at my dick since she knew she couldn't actually spray me with it. It was small, but there was a lot of force in that throw so I immediately grabbed my nuts as I hit the floor.

"Ow! What the fuck Amber?!"

"I don't care. You deserve it. Now apologize before I do it again but even harder this time," she threatened standing over me and showing that she had another bigger bottle in her other hand that she wasn't afraid to use.

"Alright! I shouldn't have gone through your stuff, but I'm glad I did because I looked up everything and now I understand you a little better. You see I even donated to the cause so put that shit down," I told her as I writhed around a bit because the pain had finally reached my stomach.

All of a sudden she looked really worried and asked if there was something she could do. It hurt so bad that I couldn't even make a joke out of asking her to rub it for me so I just had her get me a pain pill and an icepack from the freezer.

"I am so sorry. I really thought it would only hurt for a minute because men are always exaggerating about everything," she said as she helped me get up and sit on my bed.

"You mean you haven't read a book on the subject yet?" I chided her as the sharp pain finally began to subside and she smiled sheepishly. "It's okay. And since I'm being such a forgiving boss, maybe now you can forgive me too and finally explain what's going on with you?"

"First of all, we've already been through this and you're not my boss. Second, trying to explain what most doctors don't even understand is useless and just brings on more questions so I don't tell anybody about what I have."

"Alright I get that for everybody else, but how did you think I wouldn't find out when we're literally with each other all day, every day?"

"Well to be honest you're not that bright," she cracked on me. "And I figured you would just think what everybody else thinks. That I was lazy or on drugs," she said in a low voice and I immediately felt guilty because I had thought both at some point.

"Well I don't and you can talk to me about this. I mean we've been tearing down walls and opening up about everything else so why not this too?" I asked and she sighed.

"Because it's not cute or funny like you see in those movies and cartoons."

"I know. I just read about how fucked up it can be for y'all," I said trying to sympathize with her.

"That still doesn't make you an expert. Until you have to treat yourself like a fucking pin cushion just to stay awake in public then you don't know the half of it," she said holding up her scarred arms that I'd been curious about before. I had convinced myself that she had a weird form of cutting until she explained that she would scratch, pinch, or poke herself over and over to stay awake at work when the coffee or energy drinks didn't help.

"You ever fallen asleep on the subway and missed your stop?" I asked even though I didn't want to know. I had already just gotten sad when I found out about the amount of women narcoleptics who had been victims of sexual assault because of men taking advantage of their disorder.

"All the time, but a lot of people do that. Don't worry about me. I know how to take care of myself, Chris," she said dismissively probably because of all that stuff in her arsenal, but I hoped she realized that it wouldn't do her much good if she wasn't able to use it.

"Maybe when you're awake you can, but I don't want you riding anymore so I'll pay for all your Ubers from now on," I offered because if I were a woman I would rather take my chances with one man than hundreds on the train until she explained that at least there were other women on the subway who could call the police if something were to happen to her.

I immediately got an uneasy feeling in my stomach even worse than the one that had just came from getting hit in the nuts. I felt scared for her having to live life like she did especially because she was out here on her own. That made me want to know where she came from and where her family was because I couldn't just let her leave here in a couple weeks still vulnerable to the dangers of this city.

"So what's your real story, Amber? And don't try giving me any shitty cliff notes either. You know every embarrassing thing about me so give it to me straight. To start, where are your parents?"

"Dead just like yours," she said giving it to

me straight just like I'd asked and with no chaser.

"Is that how you ended up with your grandmother?" I asked and she nodded but didn't volunteer anything else so I knew that I would have to directly ask for what I wanted to know. "How did your parents die?"

"My dad got shot when my mother was pregnant with me so I never knew him, but my mother, well she was around for a little while and she was so damn fly. She ran around with niggas with money and left us with my grandmother Malenda a lot, but I'm not knocking her because she was young and didn't know that there were consequences to getting caught up with men like that," she said and I deduced that she had been a victim of wrong time, wrong place with the wrong man, but I didn't have long to ponder it because Amber was finally in the talking mood and for once in my life I just wanted to listen.

"And I know that if she had known she wouldn't have much time with us then she would've been around more because she really loved us," she said before closing her eyes like she was imagining her mother's arms wrapped around her now instead of her own.

"Who's us? You have brothers and sisters?" I asked and finally realized that we had been spending so much time focused on me that I hadn't even bothered asking her the most basic of questions. Until this very moment she was still just as much of a stranger to me as she had been the day we met.

"I have one sister or rather I had one sister. Aurora," she said and I thought she was going quiet on me again until she continued. "Growing up in the Douglass houses we were known for always having the flyest kicks and clothes because my mother did not play about us looking raggedy. And nobody ever just called us by our first names. When they saw us coming it was always 'There goes fine ass Aurora Dior and her bad ass little sister Amber Chanel'," she said with a contagious smile because seeing hers made one form on my face too.

Hers suddenly fell though right along with a few tears from her eyes as she attempted to walk out on me, but I grabbed her hand and pulled her into a warm hug. Well most of me was warm, I thought as the icepack fell to the hardwood floor and I ran my hands up her back to calm her down because she was crying so bad that she was shaking.

"Amber, what happened to Aurora?" I asked after she had finally stopped sniffling and sobbing her eyes out. I had never really looked at them like this before, but in this moment her eyes were telling me a story of a woman that had lived several lives and each one was harder than the last. They were sad with a couple tired bags to boot from sleepless nights, but they were still nice to look at and get lost in how I was now.

"Nobody knows. They found her in a dumpster in Queens, just thrown away like she was trash. I knew that she had gotten into hooking after she met this dude who took her in after my grandmother put her out, but nobody knew his real name or even where he lived and the cops only pretended to care for a little while because her case made the news," she said and it now made sense why she was even more upset at the cop we'd encountered in the park before she continued.

"But she was more than just some young prostitute how the papers made her out to be. She was fine ass Aurora Dior, my sister and my protector. Neither of us knew what the hell narcolepsy was then, but she knew we both got sleepy all of a sudden sometimes so she taught me to never be alone with boys. And that if I felt myself getting tired when I was out to go lock myself in the nearest bathroom and lie down in front of the door just in case. And I swear just that one little piece of advice from her has saved my ass on too many occasions to count. I'm only still here because she went through everything first then did anything she could to make sure that I wouldn't have to," she said before she broke down crying again and told me that she'd been alone in this world ever since Aurora had died.

I laid us down then held her close to my chest and told her that everything would be okay. I said that even though I hadn't known her for a full two weeks yet that she had already made a difference in my life and that I would always be there for her even when this thing we were doing was over. That's when her beautiful smile peeked through her tears again and she chuckled.

"I already told you not to go falling in love with me, Chris."

"Trust me. Nobody is falling for your *Nutcracker* ass, Amber. I'm just touched by your story and maybe getting a little dopey from the pain medicine," I joked before thinking about how funny it would be if we were somehow soulmates or something stupid like that because we had definitely gotten off on the wrong foot for it to ever work. "But wouldn't that be something like out of one of your little Fabio books?"

"Nah. *The Beauty and The Incel* doesn't really have a nice ring to it and I just read love stories. I don't actually want to be in one," she informed me as she wiped her last tears and I didn't blame her after hearing how so many different men had negatively affected her life already.

"But I thought deep down all women wanted that fairytale, knight in shining armor shit," I said thinking of Tillar and the ball Cam threw for her and how even Gram's old ass who had sworn off men decades earlier because of my no good grandfather was impressed by it.

"Not me. Don't forget that *Bluebeard* was a fairytale too and he was the original incel," she joked and I laughed but still tried to convince her that she should give it a shot if she met somebody she liked. "No. The fact that you men think loving and being decent to one woman is some unrealistic fairytale tells me all I need to know about y'all so I've completely opted out of the race."

"So you really don't date or anything?" I asked in disbelief as she swore that she didn't. "C'mon do not try to tell me you're a virgin, Amber."

"I'm definitely not a virgin and even though I don't date, I do call this guy Gareth a few times a year when I…you know want to feel normal for a change," she said honestly, but all I could focus on was the nigga's name.

"Gareth? What kind of name is that?" She shrugged.

"I don't know. The name his mother gave him."

"So why him? Was he your first or your best?" I asked curiously.

"Neither, but he's the only guy that ever

stopped and waited for me when I felt tired during sex," she said nonchalantly, but I felt myself getting angry again knowing that even though she might not have looked at it that way, she had been taken advantage of by men that she'd trusted.

I didn't want to harp on that and make her cry again though so I asked her what she would do after she moved on from here in a couple weeks with the extra money in her pocket. She shrugged again.

"Survive like I've been doing. When I ran away at seventeen I thought for sure that I would be dead by eighteen just like my sister so I've been living on borrowed time for the last decade," she said and it made me realize that she was probably the only person in Manhattan more alone than I was.

I yawned because I was finally getting sleepy, but I refused to give in to the urge because I was enjoying lying in bed with and getting to know bad ass Amber Chanel.

"So the caterpillar thing is why you never laugh all the way. It's always like a little *ha* and that's it," I said and she made fun of me for not being able to say cataplexy.

"Yeah that's because my body like…freezes up and gets dumb weak when I laugh too hard or sneeze and I could fall if I'm standing up," she told me and I remembered how she had done just that after we were almost mugged.

I was sure that it was the least of her problems, but that was no way to live, scared to fully experience things. I knew because I could relate in my own way. And I wanted her to laugh with everything she had and to feel safe around me if nobody else. I wanted her to laugh freely knowing that I would catch her before she fell.

A notification popped up on the computer behind me so she lifted her head from my arms so that I could check on it. It was just some stupid stock market app that I followed telling me to update it. That's when she finally asked me some questions about banking and I explained as best I could because I had never talked about it with a non-banker since nobody had ever really cared. Most people were just concerned about the money and the prestige and the long hours.

"So do you think you'll quit soon?" she asked me since I had just confessed that I was worried about going back because I knew that eventually I would end up doing the same late nights and early mornings routine that I was healing from now due to her nap schedule.

"I can't. Banking is who I am."

"It should just be what you do," she said critically, but I didn't want to hear something like that even if it was true. My job and money were the biggest parts of my identity and without them I would feel like nothing.

"Yeah, but it's not though," I told her honestly and she nodded in understanding.

"I think I could do it. You know, be an investment banker," she said confidently as she looked up at me from my bed.

"Nah. I wouldn't advise anybody to take on all that comes with this life. You're tough, you're smart and you're quick on your feet. I'm sure you could be anything you want to be, but not this shit."

"You know you're the first person who ever told me that," she said softly as she sat up then leaned on her elbow and I couldn't help but notice how good she looked lying in my bed in just her pajamas. They weren't tight or revealing or anything like that, but I could still make out all the good parts.

"Word?" I asked in disbelief and she nodded. "Well you're the first person who wanted to fix my faults instead of just ignoring them or not sticking around," I told her as I climbed back into bed because it felt good knowing that she saw something in me that others didn't.

"Well the money definitely makes it easier," she cracked. "But you see what happens when you're nice to people and let them in? It's reciprocated," she yawned out as she rolled on her side on her Goldilocks tip because she was sleeping in my bed again.

"You going back to sleep?" I asked with a yawn of my own.

"If I can, yeah. You?"

"If you stay with me, yeah," I said before reaching over and closing my laptop for good.

After that night she started *accidentally* falling asleep in my bed or near me more often, but I didn't lie about mine because when I felt like it I would purposely go get in bed with her and Keith because it felt good waking up next to a woman that I actually liked for a change. Not liked like that obviously, but just generally liked.

And after learning about her past I felt an even bigger sense of duty to protect her since it seemed like nobody besides Aurora had ever looked out for her before. I wasn't sure what would happen when we went our separate ways soon, but I knew for the rest of our time together that I would make this an experience to remember for her too because she maybe needed it more than I did.

♛

I hadn't had *good* homemade meals this regularly since before Gram went to the home so when Amber woke me up early that morning to take her food shopping, I jumped right up and got ready.

Most of the chivalry stuff she had been teaching me these past few days I already knew from my dad, it being common sense or seeing other men do it, but I liked her showing me because she looked comfortable and confident bossing me around and she was really in her element.

It was Thursday, but she still insisted on doing Taco Tuesday since we had slept that day away the other day. She wanted to do something different though and settled on making jerk chicken tacos and fried plantains.

I had even been doing my part to help her at meal times because she mostly prepped a lot at once since it was cheaper to cook a big batch of food. She also did it for safety reasons because she only turned on the stove when she had energy in fear of starting a fire. She made lots of hearty soups and stews, things that were easy to make, cost-efficient, and they could simmer for hours without burning even if she did somehow fall asleep. Already I had gained a few pounds since she'd been here, but I wasn't complaining because I was getting some of the best food and sleep of my life.

And I didn't want to read into it too much, but a few times while we were walking Keith in the park, we had nearly gotten separated in those busy sections so we had held hands to stay together. And lately almost everywhere we went together we were doing it even if we'd left Keith at home. But I swear it wasn't like a romantic thing at all. It was just something we did without thinking because we were still cracking jokes on each other all the time and she still called me an idiot every chance I said something dumb, but we were friendlier overall since we had begun opening up more.

But I knew Chase wouldn't understand the whole platonic hand holding thing so when I spotted him walking towards us while Amber looked for the Scotch bonnets she needed, I quickly dropped her hand and fake sneezed into my elbow. She instinctively said *bless you* before she saw Chase and realized it was a real one.

"Wassup? What y'all doing here?" he asked me as he leaned over to see what was in our cart.

"Nothing. Just picking up some shit for dinner."

"You've been cooking?" he asked me surprised knowing how much I hated it despite being good at it. I told him not much, but I'd been helping her do it. "Really? You don't look like the cooking type," he said to Amber and I chuckled because even though it was true, this nigga was always saying shit that other people thought but would never actually say out loud. She just shrugged.

"Well Chris buys everything and I make him wash all the dishes so I don't mind," she said causing Chase to give me another peculiar look about that. "Hey Chase, why don't you come have dinner with us?" Amber asked to my surprise trying to be nice to him for a change.

"Thanks, but I've got plans tonight," he said before recommending a spice blend from his cart to her for the plantains in ours and being nice to her in return.

Right after he had walked away, I excused myself from her to go speak with him in private a couple aisles over. He was already standing like he knew I was going to come and explain myself.

"Nigga life coach my ass. Admit it. That's your fucking girlfriend," he said laughing at me, but I denied it all even though I understood why he thought that. "Yeah she is. Since when do you food shop or hold hands with bitches? I'm the only Logan who likes to squeeze his own produce."

"Since when do you fuck cartoon characters?" I asked him as a weak retort because it was the first thing that came to mind.

"What are you talking about?"

"Nicole. You forgot to tell me about that?" I accused before he kissed his teeth and waved me off.

"Man fuck that girl. That wasn't nothing," he spat bitterly so I knew there was a story there, but I wasn't particularly interested. I just wanted to deflect from what he'd seen me doing with Amber.

"And neither is this," I told him definitively before going back over to Amber only now I had put my hands in my pocket before she could reach for one, but she didn't even bother.

"Chris, are you embarrassed to be seen with me?" she asked me while looking straight in my face.

"Why would you say that?" I asked hoping that she hadn't heard the conversation I'd just had with Chase.

"Because this is the second time you've acted like that when somebody you knew saw us together. First in your office with Kemp and now this," she said and I just put my head down and sighed.

"It's not you. I'm embarrassed that I'm doing shit that I said I would never do with you. Shit that I clowned my brothers for all of our lives."

"Well they're gonna see it eventually when you get serious with somebody for real, right?" she asked and I nodded as I tried to take her hand again, but she stubbornly claimed not to want it anymore so instead I hugged her from behind and kissed her neck.

"Am I doing this right?" I asked even though I felt the way her body relaxed in my arms.

"Yeah you're a real natural, stupid," she said and when I saw that she had closed her eyes I made her open them because I thought she was getting sleepy. "Nah I'm fine, but thank you," she told me as she brought her hand up to rub my face right as Chase came back to our aisle and I sighed.

"Don't mind me. I forgot to get my peppers," he said smugly because I didn't bother letting her go this time.

By the time we were home and getting started on cooking, Chase had already snitched and told Gram that I had a new girlfriend and that she was living with me. I tried to explain that Amber was just a friend that I was helping out, but she didn't believe me and began the inquisition.

"Christian, are you in a relationship?" she asked me through a FaceTime call. She loved to do that with us to prove how cool she was even though it had taken me hours to teach her how to do it.

"No I'm not. I mean I guess you could say kind of, but it's an experiment," I said looking over at Amber who was chopping the onions and not paying me any attention. Keith, who was usually always by my side when I was home was over by her feet because since Amber had gotten here she was always wherever she was even waiting outside the bathroom for her.

"You young people have so many ways to avoid saying you like someone. Friends with benefits, hooking up, on the down low. Are you on the down low with this young woman?" she joked mocking us and I laughed.

"On the down low doesn't mean the same thing anymore, Gram," I quipped before she asked what it meant now, but I just kept laughing at her.

"Well let me go to the google and find out for myself," she said before her screen went black and all I heard was her voice. "Oh my lord!" she said and I imagined her clutching her chest and I laughed harder.

"Christian, you know there's nothing you could ever do to make me stop loving you. And my church is much more accepting these days so you can even bring *him* to service on Sunday sometimes," she said genuinely trying to be understanding of my "boyfriend", but I was laughing so hard now that I finally got Amber's attention.

"I'm not on the down low, Gram and church isn't really *her* thing, but to get you off my back I'll see if she wants to have brunch with us after and please don't embarrass me."

"Now when have I ever embarrassed you?" she asked, but I told her that there wasn't enough time in the day to list everything. "Well nevermind then. But is she there now with you?" Gram asked hopefully and I looked over at Amber who was shaking her head and gesturing that she would hit me in the balls again if I said yes.

"No, that's just my new chef Lucy," I lied trying to protect the family jewels from Amber's wrath.

"I know when you're lying to me, Christian. It's been a long time, but don't think you're too old to be put over my good knee," she said with her same old threat. "Anyway I look forward to seeing you Sunday, young lady," she said to Amber before ending the call.

I'd had jerk tacos before but never any as spicy and tasty as these were so I gave my compliments to the chef after eating and washing the dishes.

"That's because you've been eating that bland white people stuff outside at the food truck by the office," Amber cracked on me from the couch as she rubbed Keith's belly and I agreed that I could never go back to enjoying those now.

"So I know you already heard, but let me formally invite you to brunch with me and my Gram on Sunday. It's at Chase's restaurant so his girl might be there too," I told her as a heads up because I didn't really get along with Parker, but in this case it wasn't just me since she didn't seem to get along with anybody not even Chase.

"Why does she want to meet me?"

"Hell if I know because I told her we're not together for real."

"Well I'll go because after trying that plantain recipe I do want to see Chase's menu. But your grandmother better be nice to me because I have no problem fighting senior citizens so she needs to keep her Life Alert button close enough for comfort," she joked and we both laughed hard until she suddenly tensed up.

I knew it was just the cataplexy, but I still went over and moved Keith out of the way so that I could hold her until her muscles relaxed again. That led to us *platonically* cuddling on the couch, channel surfing and shit talking.

"I know you said that you don't want to date or get married, but you would actually make a decent wife one day," I said trying to mess with her about all of her positive home related qualities because I knew she would take it as a backhanded compliment.

"Gee thanks sir!" she said sarcastically.

"I mean it though. Cam just married a woman who can barely boil water and has him cooking for her."

"Maybe that's not where his priorities are. And what's wrong with him cooking for her?" she asked going into feminist mode as she sat up.

"Well she could stand to skip a meal or two if you know what I'm saying," I said honestly which earned me a pinch from her.

"Why do you think you have the right to be so critical of women's bodies? You're getting pretty thick yourself now so your suits are gonna be a smidge too small and you're already a little pigeon toed incel."

"Alright. Enough about me. I can have an opinion about her."

"Yeah a wrong one. She's doing something right because even you're jealous enough to be in your feelings over her marriage," she said matter-of-factly.

"Not really because I know I can do better than her. I want my equal and I'm not taking care of no lazy chick."

"Well your equal can see you coming and she's running in the opposite direction right now," she said before lying back down at the opposite end of the couch and digging her bare feet in between me and the couch to keep them warm.

It was a little cold in here from the central air plus I knew that she was anemic or something too so I grabbed them and put them inside my shirt to warm them up faster for her. She thanked me then asked to see a picture of Cam and Tillar.

"I knew it! They look dumb happy together, she's bad and no funny shit, but look at those titties and that jatty on her. You're a bonafide hater, Chris," she playfully accused me, but I smacked my lips because I knew she couldn't tell just from looking at them.

"How do you know they're happy for real? People fake it all the time online for likes and validation."

"Her eyes," she said simply and I didn't dispute it because even I could see it too when I looked at her and it reminded me of my dad's words.

"When a woman isn't loved right it shows on her face and in her spirit. Never be the man who doesn't love a woman right, Chris. The only thing you should take from her is the trash to the curb."

"Well I guess she's not that bad. Just dumb for believing in fairytales."

"Well she can't be too dumb. She found the one nigga willing to actually create one for her. Most of us will never know what that's like so I'm glad at least one black woman is living it."

"You don't think you're living one right now?" I asked her and she frowned at me. "What? We're practically doing a *Pretty Woman* reboot minus the sex angle. But if you change your mind and want to add that angle, I'm all in," I said playfully even though I meant it. She didn't even bother addressing it and instead began mocking me.

"Nigga, when did you see *Pretty Woman*?"

"Once on a plane," I said quickly because I knew the jokes were right around the corner.

"No, they have choices. You wanted to see that shit, didn't you?" she asked amused.

"The point is that I rescued you from a cop and from catching Hep C in that shady motel I found you in, but you're giving my love-goofy brother all the props like I'm not right here."

"You really want me to give you some props, Chris?" she said in a teasing way all of a sudden as she ran her feet back and forth from my stomach to my chest. I nodded because that shit oddly felt so good that I couldn't speak for a second. "Come over here," she told me, but I told her to come to me instead as I sat up to see what she was about to do.

She got up on her knees and crawled back over to me and I saw a quick peek of her hard, bare nipples from the loose tank she wore. She hovered over me then bent only to softly whisper in my ear, "You're slightly less of a dick than you were when we met. Happy now?" she asked with a laugh and I pushed her off of me for getting me excited for nothing.

She still came back and laid her head on my chest though and I ran my hands up her arms because she had goosebumps from the cool air. It would have made more sense to go get her a sweater or a blanket, but I preferred touching her over convenience any day.

"I guess I just don't understand why you hate Cam so much when Chase is the one who's literal garbage?" she asked me all of a sudden.

"I don't trust anybody who hasn't had a hoe phase," I said being half-serious until she sighed and made me give her a real reason. "I told you already that he left us, didn't I? We were all hurting over Cree, but he didn't care about what we were going through."

"You also told me that he lost a wife and a child at the same time. Hopefully you'll never know what that's like," she said and it made me think about my dad and all the times I'd wished that I would have died with my mother and how much worse that would've been on him. "Try to let it go."

"I have. But when this one leaves him too, I still don't want to hear from him."

"Stop being so stubborn. I hope they never break up. They make a good couple and I know their sex is popping," she said with a dreamy look in her eyes that I hoped wasn't about Cam.

"You sure you're not into girls?" I asked

curiously because picturing her going muff diving on Tillar made my dick stir in my pants more than the thought of kissing her a few minutes ago did.

"Not even a little bit, but I know chemistry when I see it," she informed me so I took her word for it. "And I know we've accepted that you're never really gonna be shit, but since we're almost at the end, can I get some answers out of you?"

"Shoot," I said giving her permission to ask me whatever.

"Okay, I hate to sound like a nigga here, but who hurt you? It doesn't seem like you've ever let a woman get close enough to…until me, but that's only because you know this isn't real so I can't actually hurt you." I sighed.

"I've been doing a lot of thinking about that too lately and maybe you weren't wrong about me still feeling guilty about my mother dying."

"Well you need to fix that shit then," she said bluntly. "You want to be miserable for the rest of your life over something you can't change?"

"It's not the end of the world that I'm fucked up because of my mother. Plenty of people are."

"No, at this point you're choosing to be fucked up, Chris. You either want a good life or you don't and living in the past isn't going to get it for you. You'd think knowing what happened to her would make you appreciate life more and try to do something with it instead of just chasing money and still being miserable."

"Well since you seem to have all the answers, tell me how I should go about doing that?" I challenged her.

"I never said I had all the answers, but your brothers didn't let not having her affect them with women so what's your problem?" I shrugged.

"Maybe they're just better at pretending than I am," I said before she was about to lay into me again. "Okay, I'll give you Cam, but Chase is just as miserable as me."

"Well maybe you need acting lessons too then because at least they have somebody. You can't even get a woman to stick around without paying her," she said not even trying to be malicious because it was the truth and I accepted it now.

"You know you should really look into being a life coach for real after this," I complimented her because as much as I had talked shit about her and those damn books, I had learned so much about myself and the world from her in this short amount of time.

"How when I'm still in the trenches my damn self?"

"I think your life experience would make you perfect for the job actually. Only people from the trenches really know how to get out of them."

"Well thanks, but after you I'm done helping niggas. Hopefully hanging around you gave me the secret to meeting a rich dude who's not such a penny pincher and then he can save me from going back to the pole for good," she said nonchalantly through a yawn, but my mouth was practically on the floor at her latest revelation.

"I knew it! So you really were a stripper before?" I asked thinking that I had caught her slipping up about her past.

"The subway pole, idiot," she said laughing before I joined in with her. "I'm tired of taking the subway. Tired of working. Shit I'm tired of life period," she yawned out.

"You feeling suicidal?" I asked thinking that we were still playing around, but she didn't answer until I repeated the question.

"It's not exactly like I have much to live for."

"You have plenty to live for," I said instead of giving her something concrete because I was stumped too. But I knew she had to have some purpose other than providing me with some much needed company and a nap buddy lately.

"Like what? To pay bills? I don't even get to escape during sleep like most people. And if I did off myself then at least I could finally get some much needed rest," she joked morbidly until she saw me frown. "I'm not talking about right now,

Chris."

"When then?" I asked since apparently she was serious about this.

"I don't know," she said softly as she looked down at the bruises on her arm again.

"Well when's the last time you thought about it then?" I asked curiously and she looked up at me and smiled widely.

"When you got me fired from Bean."

"Seriously?" I asked feeling like shit.

"Yeah. I was finally ready to take the great big nap, but I got back to the hotel room and I was too exhausted to do it so I just took a regular nap instead," she said earnestly but still lightheartedly enough that I didn't feel bad about laughing.

"Well don't go doing anything drastic just yet. At least wait until after I get my promotion so I can get sympathy points," I said before saying what I really wanted to say to her. "For real though, Amber. I need you to stick around because paid or not I don't have any other friends. And I didn't realize how lonely I was until you got here," I said being more honest than I'd intended on being as she looked up at me and agreed with the sentiment.

"So what happens when you move out then? We'll still hang out sometimes, right?" I asked her trying not to sound desperate for her attention.

"Just when I want to see my baby," she said as she put her hand across my stomach so Keith could lick it. "You better watch her closely before I steal her because you do not deserve such a good doggy."

"Don't get any ideas. I have a tracker implanted on her and I'll find you and I'll kill you," I said doing my best Liam Neeson in *Taken* impression.

"Dammit. Whatever I'm sure I'll see you running through the park like a Bozo at some point. I might wave if I'm not with my rich husband. You better act like you don't know me if I am though," she joked and for some reason hearing her speaking about being with another man made me…not jealous but *jealous* for lack of a better word.

I'd seen firsthand how she had charmed my boss and the other VPs and she definitely had it in her to land somebody less shallow than me because she was cute and spunky and niggas with money liked cute and spunky. I was even starting to come around to the idea of it.

⚜

Church went a little long, but it still flew by that Sunday and before I knew it, it was time to meet Amber for brunch with Gram. I had offered to swing back by my building to pick her up, but she said she'd grab a taxi and meet us at the restaurant for convenience.

I wasn't surprised to see her already there and drinking coffee when Gram and I arrived because I was starting to recognize her triggers and I could see her getting tired before it happened. She was good and as well rested as she could be today though, just a little nervous about meeting Gram for some reason even though I had told her that Gram would be nice to her face even if she didn't actually like her because she was phony like that.

We were running late and it was packed in there so our usual table had been given away and Amber was seated at a table near the restroom. I had to pee bad anyway from sitting there hearing that screaming pastor for the last three hours so after introducing them I headed that way.

But when I was coming back to the table I heard them talking about me from behind the wall that separated the washrooms from the dining area.

"Lately Christian has been making changes that, quite frankly, I really like. Am I wrong to assume those changes are due to your presence in his life?" Gram asked Amber not even attempting to beat around the bush.

"I guess you could say that. We've been

helping each other out in different ways. He gave me a place to stay and I've been helping him be more...well nice."

"I can see. You know, last year I was really worried about my Cameron getting engaged too soon, but everything turned out just fine with his wife Tillar. The fact that I have absolutely no reservations about you and my Christian is concerning to me because usually when something seems too good to be true it is," she said and I couldn't wait to hear how Amber answered the assumption that we would end up together.

"Ms. Ida, Chris has been there for me like nobody else for the short time that I've known him and I appreciate that more than I could ever tell him. He's a special man and I know what you're getting at here, but I've seen too much of the old him to know that he's not the man for me and we're better off as friends," she told her respectfully.

"Is it because you're not convinced that the changes will last?"

"I'm not sure, but to be honest I'm not willing to take the risk because past behavior predicts future behavior. He's definitely not ready for something real right now and I'm not sure if he ever will be because he's hurting inside and I'm still trying to figure out why. As a friend I'm willing to be there for him in any way I can, but I know ultimately it's up to him to fix him," she said and that's when I decided to come back to the table because I didn't want to hear anymore.

They both put on fake smiles over the meal and had great small talk, but I was short for the rest of brunch and stayed in my phone until it was time to drop Gram back off at the home. The whole time I had been thinking of returning those stupid ass expensive Chanel bags that I had picked out for Amber and hid in my hall closet, but I knew I wouldn't because I did still want to see her reaction when I would give them to her on our last night together. She wouldn't be expecting one let alone three so it would be the perfect gesture to end things.

I knew that Amber had sensed something was wrong with me, but she wasn't going to bring it up so I did the honors the second I came back from walking Gram inside.

"I heard your little heart to heart with my Gram. So you really think I'm damaged beyond repair?"

"Those are your words, Chris, not mine," she said passively.

"So what this is just a money grab for you for real? I thought we were actually becoming friends here."

"We are friends and if you were actually

listening then you would have heard me tell her that. Why are you mad when you know you don't want me either?" she asked sounding annoyed.

"Because it's not about wanting you, Amber. A real friend wouldn't say no shit like you just did about me," I complained even though there were certainly remnants of truth to what she'd said.

"Really? Because from day one you've made it perfectly clear that I don't meet your bougie ass, catalog standards, but now you're bothered because I said you don't meet mine either?" she asked accusing me of being a hypocrite, but I didn't care about that shit anymore.

"Why would it never work between us?" I asked curiously even though I had my own fair share of reasons. I just wanted to hear hers though.

"Well aside from the obvious incel elephant in the room, why does it even matter to you?" she asked and I wanted to tell her that it was because I just wanted to know what she was thinking sometimes.

She was a straight shooter and seemed to say whatever came to mind, but it never seemed to be what I wanted to hear. I wanted to know the thoughts that she kept to herself, the ones that she would never share with anybody.

"I guess it doesn't really matter," I said

trying to not sound too invested and she used it as an excuse to drop the conversation altogether.

We stubbornly went our separate ways when we got back to the apartment, but after getting changed into regular clothes I knocked on her door then barged in because I had something else to say. She was stepping into a pair of pants so I caught a glimpse of her smooth, bare brown legs and thighs and the underwear she was wearing. I ignored that though because I had a point to make.

"Okay we got Reisman in the bag and I'm the most well-read nigga on feminism in this metropolis so for this last week fuck those books. I need you to show me how to do the real life romantic shit for real because I told you from the beginning that field experience is what I need."

"But you know dating isn't really my area of expertise."

"Mine either so I guess we're gonna figure this shit out together."

"What's there to learn? Open her door, pull out her chair, don't talk about your dick, then pick up the check. You got this, champ," she said sarcastically as she patted my shoulder.

"No. Starting tonight, we're going out every night until you leave so take that shit back off and go put on a dress," I told her instead of asking her because these were my new conditions.

She nodded like she agreed, but after searching the closet for a minute she came back and said she had to lie down first. I wasn't buying this act at all though. I had already peeped her doing this to get out of stuff she didn't want to do a few days ago.

"Amber Chanel, you're not getting out of this so get your ass up," I said as I nudged her and she laughed.

"How did you know I was faking?" she asked as she sat up in bed.

"Because you got up," I quipped then told her to be ready in fifteen minutes because we were starting our final chapter together and this was going to be the good shit.

6

LOSING SLEEP

I finally took advantage of my Junior VP perks for Amber's and my date nights because there was always free shit, gifts, and tickets passed on from the Senior VPs and managing directors. I took her to see *Hamilton* on Broadway and she loved it even though she fell asleep a couple times throughout.

I made her get really dressed up again when we went to a symphony at Carnegie Hall. But she was over that type of shit by the third night and insisted on doing regular folks date stuff like bowling and going to the movies because she was always worried about fitting in even though she always looked the part.

Obviously she had never been anywhere nice for dinner because she always looked up the menu beforehand to make sure she could pronounce everything, but I told her that she was ruining half the fun of getting told the specials.

We went shopping at Bergdorfs and hung

out in Columbus Circle and held hands just like a real couple and I had to admit that I had begun to look forward to our "dates". Neither of us had ever experienced any of this before and it was just something we'd both seen in the movies. But it was all about practice and in a weird way I was glad that I was the one to do these firsts for her because they were firsts for me too and we would both leave with the knowledge we were learning about dating.

My time had always been worth a lot of money to me, but I didn't feel like I was wasting it with her how I used to back when I wasn't working on weekends. During our free time I liked to listen to her talk about her life because she had lots of funny stories despite not having a good childhood.

She had more sad ones too though like how she had come to love the library so much because it was literally her home for a few months after she'd ran away since a kind woman who worked overnight security let her stay there until she got on her feet. We had actually grown up maybe fifteen minutes away from each other, but it seemed like completely different worlds and I wanted to do what I could to make the rest of her life better, you know as a friend who cared about her a lot.

And I especially appreciated her for coming

with me to my dad's house with me and Chase to finally pack up his stuff. I still didn't want to let it go or let strangers have it, but at the same time I knew I wanted more than what living there represented so I was finally coming around to giving in to the pressure from Gram, Cam and Chase.

On our last Saturday together we had gone to the Statue of Liberty because even though she grew up in the city, she had never been to tourist hotspots like that.

"You mean you didn't even go on field trips back then?" I asked her in disbelief after we had climbed to the top to see the beautiful view of the water.

"We couldn't afford it so my grandma never let us go places," she said before telling me that she hadn't even gone to the movies until she could afford it herself at nineteen.

"What did you go see?" I asked curiously.

"Some action bullshit that I fell asleep on, but what I did see was magical and I felt normal for the first time in my life."

She knew that I hated amusement parks and boardwalks something serious, but since we only had one more day before I had to report back to work, I suggested taking her to Coney Island because she had never been there either. She did a double take to make sure that she'd heard me right.

"Wow. I think my work here is done, Chris. You're now considerate enough to do things that you know you'll hate just to please a woman," she said laughing but clarified that she was serious about being done.

"Are you sure you don't want to keep playing pretend with me? I still don't think I'm ready for the real thing yet," I said in a playful voice.

"Well your thirty days is over tomorrow and you're as ready as you're gonna be. It's really just common sense at this point, but you can call me if you need advice about something," she assured me before finally telling me that she had an interview at another coffee shop on Monday so naturally I inquired about where so that I could pop up on her sometimes.

"I'm not telling you because I want to keep this one and I wouldn't put it past you to get me fired again." I smiled because that was the second thing that had come to mind. "You don't need me anymore, Chris. Your boss buys the new you act and you know if you need a date for something work related before you find your real life black Barbie in the catalog that I'll go with you," she said and I thanked her for offering to keep this going overtime if need be.

"Well have you found a new roommate yet

since you got everything else figured out already?"

"Not yet, but I'm checking out a place tomorrow," she told me proudly. And of course I knew she wouldn't stay forever, but she had stricken me as the type that I would have to formally evict after enforcing squatter's rights or something. I immediately volunteered to go with her before realizing that she was scheduled to go when I would be at church with Gram.

"I'm glad everything is falling into place for you too, but just for the record you know you can stay as long as you need, right? I like having you there with me," I told her honestly.

"So does this mean that you're gonna miss me, Chris?" she asked in a sing-song voice and I couldn't even pretend that I wouldn't.

"Hell yeah and I'd gladly hire you as my chef. It'll come with free room and board for you," I joked but saw her scrunch up her face a little at the comment.

"I'm good. And I don't know how to make that bougie food you like."

"Good because I like your food better anyway," I complimented her before trying something else. "Okay no cooking then, but I know you clean good too so what about being my maid? I could even get you one of those little French outfits and watch you dust on weekends,"

I said flirtatiously, but she full on frowned at my joke this time.

"I would rather go skinny dipping in the Hudson in December."

"Okay okay, what about this? No cooking or cleaning, but you love Keith and I know you don't want her to be alone again all day when I go back to work so how about you just be my live-in dog walker or something like that for her? C'mon just stay, Amber," I shamelessly begged her, but she shook her head no.

"Your time is up, rich boy. I need to get back to focusing on me."

"But you can do that with me and you'll practically have the whole place to yourself because of my hours," I offered, but her answer remained the same. "Wait a minute. I know what this is," I said trying to sound serious.

"You know what 'what' is?"

"The reason you're trying to get away from me is because you've fallen for all this new drip and charm you taught me, right?" I asked and she laughed so hard I prepared for her to tense up, but she didn't.

"Oh please. Falling for a man like you is the height of stupidity, Chris. But you have been a pretty good friend so maybe the woman who ends up with you won't be so doomed after all. Just glad it won't be me," she said and as much as I hated to admit it, it was like a dagger to the chest because I was sure that I had done a good job as a pretend boyfriend this past week.

The next morning I woke up to Amber and Keith already on the couch being lazy bums. She had a hard time going to bed last night, but she wanted to be alone so she had slept in her own bed for the first time in a while.

"You sure you don't want to come to church with me? It's the first Sunday and niggas will be in there ripe for jokes," I told her as I headed for the door.

"No. I really don't want to spend my birthday in church," she said casually before a yawn.

"It's your birthday today?! Why didn't you tell me?" I asked excitedly, but she just shrugged her shoulders.

"Because it's just another day," she said nonchalantly and while I didn't know her exact reasoning I understood what she meant.

Gram and my dad had tried to make mine feel special each year growing up, but I didn't like celebrating because I couldn't ignore that it was my mother's death anniversary too. And most people would probably think the idea of missing somebody that they'd never met was impossible, but I yearned for her especially on that day.

"Okay well fuck, Happy Birthday! And we'll

do something fun when I get back," I promised as I kissed the top of her head then covered her up with a blanket because I knew she would get cold eventually.

Instead of looking around at the people who only came on the first Sunday of the month, I thought that I would be focused on going back to work tomorrow, but with Amber going apartment hunting today I had gotten ahead of myself with premature excitement about finally having somebody to come home to after long days. I tried to trick myself into believing that it was mostly about her homecooked meals, but I accepted the truth because she was my friend now and it was okay to care about or even miss a friend. If I could still miss my mother, then I could definitely miss Amber.

I was as full as a tick by the time I got home from church and brunch with Gram, but Amber had the house smelling so good that I knew I wanted a few bites of whatever she was making. I saw her from behind standing over the stove and despite telling me through text that she actually preferred to stay in tonight, she was still dressed nice.

"You know you shouldn't be cooking for your birthday. I was gonna take you somewhere," I said because I had been wracking my brain for a spot all day since her palate was so damn limited.

We hadn't been to Catch Steak yet so I was leaning towards there because even though it had gotten trendy lately, it was still a decent steak that was close by and I knew she would like it.

"I don't mind. You know I only really like my food. You rich people spend all that money just to be seen in those joints 'cause you know that shit don't be good," she said making me laugh thinking about her giving her leftovers to Keith then making grilled cheeses when we got home.

I looked in the big pot on the stove and saw that the good smells were coming from oxtails that had been simmering for a while. She sent me looking for the spice that Chase had given her in the pantry, but I couldn't find it so she got it herself.

"If it was a snake it would've bit you," she told me sarcastically and I smiled because it was true.

"You sound just like my Gram."

"Mine too," she said softly which surprised me after everything I'd learned about that woman. I watched her add in a little more salt too before cutting me off a tender little bite with a fork and placing it near my mouth.

"Damn that's good," I almost moaned at how the meat melted in my mouth.

"I'm glad you like it because this might be your last big meal from me. The place I saw today was cool and I'm gonna take it," she said as she put the lid back on the pot.

"When can I see it?" I asked instead of reminding her once again that she could stay longer because I didn't want to come off clingy.

"Never," she quipped. "There's not much to see anyway. It's not like here with all the waitlists and applications and shit. It's just a place that seems like it could be home for a little while."

"Sounds perfect for you. And since it's your birthday, it's about time that I give you a little something for you to put in your new closet."

"What?" she asked as she put down the fork. Her eyes lit up when I came back with the black Chanel shopping bag that I'd pulled from the closet.

"You know I went in there to get the cheapest one, but all of these had you written all over them," I told her as I handed it to her and she screamed with joy as she saw not one, but three Chanel shoulder bags and the check I'd written for her. I laughed out loud when she called me the Feds for not paying her in cash especially since I had given her more than what we'd agreed on to make sure she would be good financially for a while after she moved out.

"Nig-ga! I can't believe you really tricked off this much for me! What is the world coming to?!" she laughed out excitedly.

"Alright. Calm down. TI said it wasn't tricking if you got it and we both know I got it."

"TI is a tricking ass lie, but thank you so much, Chris!" she exclaimed again as she sat everything down then wrapped her arms around my neck. Instinctively my hands fell to her hips before returning the friendly hug.

And I didn't know if it was just the heat from us standing so close to the stove, but when she finally pulled back from the warm embrace she laid a juicy kiss on me. I was caught off guard at first, but I didn't let it slow me down because I grabbed the back of her neck and slobbed her down until she eventually ended it to catch her labored breath. I could've gone on longer, I thought as I tapped her trembling lips a few more times with mine and watched her chest heave up and down.

"What was that about?" I asked her still holding onto her by the waist.

"Is this starting to feel a little too real to you too?" she asked sounding unsure which was unusual for her. I nodded as I licked my lips because I still wanted to taste hers again.

"That's because it is real. Our friendship is real and that kiss was definitely real. But good thing we know this would never work so we're keeping that shit in check, right?" I said and she quickly agreed before I let go of her and leaned on the counter. "But a pterodactyl like you would start acting like you like me for real after I gave you those bags," I mumbled and she laughed at me calling out her big, ancient bird behavior.

"I do not like you like that, Chris. You just have quick glimpses of a decent dude peeking out sometimes," she said then got serious all of a sudden. "So I talked to your grandma after you dropped her off and she asked me if I could try to get you to call Cam."

I smiled then told her that Gram had been doing her best to make us talk since the wedding, but I'd respected his wishes when he said that he didn't want shit else to do with me. And I guess a part of me also didn't want to talk to him until I had something better than what he had too.

When we were done eating and pretending like we hadn't kissed, she got up to do the dishes because she saw how full I looked, but I made her sit back down.

"No you definitely shouldn't be cooking and washing dishes on your birthday. I'll do them," I said then told her to go play with her bags.

"Thanks," she said before helping herself to more wine that we'd had for the meal.

I was almost done washing everything when she came up and hugged me tightly from behind.

"Thank you again, Chris...for everything,"

she said sincerely, but all I could focus on was how much I liked how her arms felt around my waist.

"It was nothing."

"No, all of this was definitely something," she said as she planted a kiss in the middle of my back and I shivered.

"What are you doing back there?" I asked peering over my shoulder at her.

"Pretending you're my rich husband for real just for tonight," she said in a low, teasing voice and I swear my dick had never gotten harder in my life.

"You better get off me unless you want me to expect what rich husbands expect on nights like this," I joked even though I loved how her breasts felt pressed up against my back. During the meal I had already seen her stiff nipples pressing through the thin fabric of her dress, but I ignored it by focusing on her face instead how she'd taught me to do when I was eventually out with a real date.

"Well maybe I should pretend harder then so that I can give you exactly what you're expecting," she said as her hands began their trek from my waist to the front of my pants. I was too stunned to moan when she cupped my dick and I thought that maybe I had somehow caught her cataplexy because I was now frozen solid where I stood.

I finally turned to face her to make sure she wasn't playing some cruel trick on me again, but when I saw that yearning in her eyes I knew that she really did want this too. And although I was more than full from the delicious meal she'd prepared, all of a sudden I was craving something sweet that I'd never had before.

"Since we're pretending that you're my wife tonight, can I do something that I've been saving just for her?" I asked because I had been getting hard for weeks just thinking about letting her take a ride on my face. I guess the thought of that appealed to her too because she closed her eyes and gave me permission to do it as she bit her lip then ran my hand up the side of her thigh so that I could feel she wasn't wearing any panties. Fuck.

She had planned this, I thought as she led me over to her room and for the first time she left a confused Keith on the other side as she closed the door.

She kissed me hard and barely wanted to let go of my lips when I laid her down, but I made her then prepared to put mine on her other lips.

"You really haven't done this before?" she asked looking up at me after I'd asked for instructions on how she wanted it done. I shook my head no then began kissing lower because it was long overdue. "Okay it's really not that hard.

Just focus on my clit and pretend like you're sucking and licking a tiny dick," she said graphically and I laughed.

"Alright, nevermind," I joked because I had thought about this damn near every day for the past month so I knew I wasn't getting up without her leaving her flavor on my taste buds.

"That's cool. Just know you're never getting wifed without learning how to do it," she said because she had believed me about not wanting to do it anymore.

"First of all. I'm a man so nobody is *wifing* me anyway," I told her as I lifted her dress above her waist which made me forget my second point because I was mesmerized at the sight of the neatly shaven pussy that was now in my face. So she wasn't one of *those* feminists, I thought as I licked my lips.

"What are you waiting for? Kiss her," she said impatiently while looking in my eyes and I swear I almost came right then and there. I did just like she said and held eye contact as she further instructed me to also use my fingers.

"Like this?" I asked trying to seem more clueless than I was as I curled them to reach her inner soul and she responded by arching her back and moving up towards the headboard. "Get back here. I can't learn if you're running," I told her as I chased after her pussy and slurped on the already running juices.

"Mm. Are you sure you haven't done this before?" she moaned out, but I didn't answer because my mouth was now too busy experiencing total bliss to say anything.

I continued following her instructions, but I also went with what felt natural as I licked to the beat of her pulse. I watched what made her back arch even more than it already was and I did that some more until she locked her legs around my head and tensed up so bad that I had sent her into a cataplexy spell. I didn't mind being stuck though and I kept sucking her clit until she relaxed again and let me go.

"I did good?" I asked her sarcastically and she laughed at me then grabbed her pussy like she was making sure that it was still there or something.

"Yeah. My bad I should have warned you about that," she yawned out about freezing up, but I had taken it as a compliment to my natural skillfulness.

"You're not too feminist or too sleepy to return the favor, are you?" I asked her after lying down next to her and she grinned at me as she got up.

And as much as I would have loved to pretend that I lasted longer than I did, I wasn't gonna even lie about it. I came quick as hell after seeing Amber hungrily drag her wet, warm mouth up and down the shaft of my dick. And I wasn't even ashamed because I had just gone thirty days without feeling a woman and that shit had been building up in me.

I saw a flash of worry in her eyes that I was always a quick nutter, but I had a magic trick to show her and I did as my dick remained hard in her mouth even after coming. I reached over in my drawer to get a condom because now that I had that first nut out of the way, I was ready to show her how I got down.

I had figured that this first time would be a standard missionary kind of thing especially because she looked pretty tired, but after sliding it on for me she laid me back down then saddled up to ride. And I let her because I knew that some of her past sexual experiences had left her feeling like she wasn't in control of her body and I wanted that for her with me.

The hot, wet grip that I felt as she lowered herself on me felt like the nerves in my dick were suddenly attending a fireworks show. I tried to thrust upwards as much as I could from this position, but after a while I relaxed and let her control the speed that was most comfortable to her. With her eyes closed and her teeth dangerously gnawing into her bottom lip, she rolled her hips in the shape of an oval until I finally shifted and hit a spot so tender that her eyes flew open.

"Right there?" I asked her pointlessly as I grabbed hold of her hips and held her tightly in place as I fucked her with everything I had in me in that moment. She instantly howled and trembled like a junkie as she came and I could have sworn that I wasn't even close to finishing until her sweet walls began contracting around me and milking me like I was livestock.

Without warning, she had suddenly fallen asleep on top of me and I just laid there, still buried deep inside of her as I caught my breath and tried to come down from the high I was on. I couldn't make myself think about anything other than the fact that I wanted to do that every day for the rest of my life.

A few minutes later, I felt her coming back to life and waking up. She lifted her head from my chest then looked down at me before I latched onto her lips again.

"Wait. You mean that wasn't a dream like it always is? We really just did that for real?" she asked me in a tired, weak voice because a nigga had just put in work.

"You dream about fucking me?" I asked amused, but she just moaned as she nodded because she was still full of me and I still wasn't all the way soft yet. She started to slowly grind on me again and I had her coming again in no time because now I fondled her breasts and used the pad of my thumb to rub circles on her sensitive clit. And I bet the nasty words of encouragement I gave her didn't hurt things either.

Finally exhausted from playing pretend wife and cowgirl, she rolled off of me and onto the bed and the condom that I'd been wearing must've went with her because my dick was slimy and wet from our mixed fluids. Before she panicked or anything spilled out, I reached over and dug it out of her.

"You're always getting something stuck in your pussy, Amber. I guess I know why now, huh?" I winked at her as I got up to get rid of it in her bathroom.

"I hate you," she said after me. "And remind me to get a Plan B tomorrow because I will not be punished by the feminist goddesses for seducing an incel," she joked before asking me when was the last time that I'd been tested.

"Every six months like clockwork, but I stay strapped regardless," I told her honestly. "And I do those full panel tests too so I have them testing me for polio and anthrax just to be sure that shit ain't came back," I exaggerated because always wrapping it up was another rule from my dad that I willingly obeyed on account of me being a gullible kid who really thought that STDs could make it fall off.

"What about you though, Brokie? When's the last time you swung by the free clinic?" I jabbed her and she playfully slapped my dick as she came into the bathroom with me to pee.

We got cleaned up in the shower together, but I didn't try anything else because I could see that she would be falling asleep soon and her alarm going off in her room proved me right. When we got out and dried off I could tell that she was trying to pretend that everything was still normal in spite of what we'd just done, but she was still tipsy and rambling about whatever came to mind.

"I'm really gonna miss this bathroom so much when I move out," she said all of sudden and I sighed because I couldn't believe that she was bringing that up now of all times.

"Amber, what is the rush? Why are you really trying to get up out of here so fast?" She shrugged.

"I guess I don't like staying in one place too long because I have a tendency to wear out my welcome," she said as she bit her lip and I grinned at her notion.

"Well that's not gonna happen anytime soon with me. In fact your performance here tonight just secured you at least six more months," I joked as I tried to kiss her again, but she dodged my lips.

"So are you saying that you really want me to stay?"

"Yeah! I've only been saying that for days now, but you ignore me every time I bring it up."

"Well because what would me staying really mean?"

"What do you mean?" I asked knowing full well what she meant, but I couldn't believe that Amber Miller was really trying to have the *what are we* talk with me. She called me out on playing dumb by just saying my name. "It means whatever you want it to mean. Just stay," I said trying to slide back into my cool façade, but she continued to pry for clarification purposes.

"But why? We both got what we needed out of the deal so what other reason do I have to stay?"

"Duh! Because we both want you to," I said hoping that she just deaded the subject altogether because I was getting irritated at what I knew she wanted me to say. She had made it perfectly clear while she was sober that she thought the idea of being with me was absurd so I knew her sudden change of heart could only mean that she was desperate or drunk or both.

"Would me staying mean that we're together for real, Chris?" she finally asked and I sighed hard as I leaned back against the sink.

"How many times have you told me that you didn't ever want to be with somebody like me?" I asked before she quickly countered.

"I don't know. Probably the same amount of times that you said you didn't ever want to be with somebody like me."

"Somebody like you? Now what is that supposed to mean?" I asked even though again, I knew what she meant. A regular, non-catalog type of woman. "Look, you shined me up as good as any woman could and you got paid damned good for it so take a bow. But you and I both know that in spite of all of this training that I'm still not in the right headspace to be with somebody right now because I still have a lot of growing up to do," I said using my Gram's words because they fit this situation perfectly.

"I still don't trust women and I know you still don't trust men, but you and me, we get each other. *We're friends* and we're honest like we've never been with anybody else. So why can't we just continue to be what we are now when you know it's better than what anybody else will offer you?" I asked her honestly, but I noticed that she couldn't even look at me anymore.

"Because it's not good enough for me," she said softly before clearing her throat and regaining her confidence. "You think that I'm gonna be okay with you eventually stumbling in at two in the morning with one of those women from the catalog? Oh and of course I wouldn't be allowed to bring a dude back here, right?" she asked bringing up a valid point, but instead of answering her I just kissed her cheek goodnight.

"This isn't you, Amber. You're drunk and temporarily dick sprung, but I swear by morning this too shall pass," I joked then headed for the door to signal that I was ending the conversation before it got out of hand even though I had really wanted to sleep next to her tonight.

I couldn't tell if I couldn't sleep because of the excitement of going back to work was on my mind or because of what Amber had said. Honestly it had caught me off guard more than anything because deep down I knew she wanted to have sex with me, but I had never considered that she wanted to *be* with me. I guess I had assumed it to be a ruse because she had gone on and on for weeks about only wanting a man with money and I was just the easiest and closest mark. That had to be it because I knew she didn't really want to move out and go back to a shithole apartment after getting used to staying here.

She was already awake and reading at the kitchen island when I came downstairs the next morning, but she hadn't made any breakfast for today. I didn't let myself think too much of that and instead just grabbed an apple and my briefcase as I noticed that she'd pulled back the curtains so the full view of the park could be seen. We hadn't done that since her first day here, but I didn't say anything about it and just appreciated how nice she looked to me in the natural morning light.

"How are you feeling?" I asked after finishing my apple and she gave a weak smile without looking up from the page.

"A little hungover, but I'll make it."

"You need me to bring you something in to make you feel better?" I asked genuinely trying to be helpful, but she declined and went back to reading so I left her alone while I finished getting ready. I decided that I would drive today because I wanted to be focused and clear-headed when I walked through the doors for the first time in a month, not sweaty and out of breath.

"What time do you think you'll be back?" she asked with her back to me as I came downstairs for the last time.

"I don't know. Late. I gotta get a little face time in with everybody to show them how mature you made me," I said playfully trying to clear the heavy air that had seemingly stuck overnight.

"Look Amber, about last night--" I began when I noticed that she still wouldn't make direct eye contact with me, but she interrupted me.

"It's cool. You are who you are, Chris. It's my fault for forgetting that we were just pretending all this time," she said as she rubbed Keith's head and I thought about how ironic it was that she had told me a few times not to fall for her, but she hadn't taken her own advice. "I did some thinking after we talked and I decided to go ahead and take the apartment so I'll probably be out of here before the end of the week," she told me in an even tone.

I checked my watch and saw that I was about to be running late so I didn't have time to get into this right now.

"I gotta go, but just please don't accept it yet. We'll figure something out when I get home later, alright?" I asked just one octave away from begging and she slowly nodded her head.

"And one more thing," I began because I felt like I should say something else, but I stopped when I saw that glimpse of hope in her eyes when hers finally met mine. "Uh…can you tell the dog walker to not be trifling for her first day back and let Keith shit on the sidewalk out front without picking it up? I got a warning the last time she was here a few weeks ago," I said and even I knew that was a stupid thing to bring up.

It wasn't until I was out the door that I realized Amber's eyes were damn near lip gloss shiny and I knew I was in trouble for real. She was gonna be crying before I made it out of the elevator. Fuck.

Why did all women have to fucking be alike? So needy and love-happy after fucking. I had really hoped that she was just loose off the goose last night, but that look in her eyes confirmed her feelings for me were getting out of control. And maybe it would be better for her to just leave now before things got too complicated.

But the thought of her living without me scared me more than I wanted to admit because I was supposed to be protecting her now. And she would need it with the neighborhoods that fit her nonexistent budget. I would have to at least convince her to stay until she let me get her a better job.

Work was work and everybody stopped by my office to tell me how rested I looked from my break. Well Lewis had used the word "clean" implying that I looked drug free, but I didn't even care because I had even missed his hating ass these last few weeks.

Under Reisman's orders I left at ten that night which was still early for me. Amber had kept popping up in my mind throughout the day, but I forced myself not to text her because I didn't want to say the wrong thing. It would have been great if I had somebody to coach me through talking to her now.

I'd gotten takeout and a bunch of the brownies she liked from Bean for her as a peace offering. Of course the food was cold now because Neal had picked it up before everything closed, but it would be fine because it was the thought that counted.

He'd also gotten a flower for her when he realized that it was for both me and Amber, but I threw that shit in the garbage the second I stepped outside the building because that would really make her wannabe aromantic ass love me.

"Bad ass Amber Chanel, c'mere! I got a double whammy for you. When you see it, you're never gonna wanna leave me again!" I announced as I came in and sat everything down, but I didn't hear anything but Keith's paws and heavy panting coming to greet me.

I figured she might've been in the bathroom and didn't hear me so I went over to her room and knocked on the door. There was no answer so I helped myself to a visitor's pass and entered anyway.

It was dark aside from the moonlight peeking through the window and the bathroom was empty too. I looked around the room for a second before turning on the light to see that everything looked the same. For a minute I thought that she had left me before I saw the Chanel bags sitting on the dresser and knew she hadn't. If she was leaving I knew she for sure wouldn't have left those behind. She was probably out fucking Gareth to make her forget about me. The thought angered me because I thought that her pussy belonged to me now, but at the same time I understood the predicament we were in so I checked myself.

But what if he was better than me? I asked myself before shaking off that thought as I got comfortable on the couch to wait up for her. I was tired, but I knew I only had until approximately the end of the week to convince her to stay so I needed to get it in her head that this could work if she just checked herself how I did whenever I was feeling jealous.

Disregarding my feelings to make it stand still, time continued to pass and at midnight I got up to eat without her. I felt like a simp having a meal meant to be shared with her while she was probably somewhere getting a belated birthday dickdown after which she would then come back to sleep in my house. And I decided that I definitely wouldn't kiss her again now that I knew what she could really do with that mouth of hers.

I fell asleep on the couch angry as hell but woke up right after dawn because I had to pee bad. I held it though as I went back to her room because I just knew she had to be home by now. She must've just been extra quiet coming in when she saw me asleep on the couch.

To my surprise she still wasn't in there and now I was getting worried so I finally gave in and texted her because she was taking this too far. Yeah she was grown, but she still should have called to say she was staying out because she knew I would worry. Shit that was probably the plan all along and I had just fallen into the simple trap she'd set.

She *wanted* me to worry so that I would in turn *want* her. Well if that was it, I wouldn't fall for it again and next time she did this I wouldn't even say shit, I thought as I went to my room to get a few more minutes of shuteye.

I was just about to piss then fall into my mattress when I saw it there. A note written on the back of a cable bill that I'd had sitting on the coffee table downstairs and underneath it were the keys I'd given her and a book called *Men Cry In The Dark*.

I wondered how long this had been there and if she had snuck in and left it all there for me. I realized that it didn't matter what time it'd been placed there when my eyes stumbled across the words *Thank you for being a friend* in her handwriting followed by her initials.

"What the fuck?" I asked aloud to no one in particular because this wasn't *The Golden Girls* and last time I checked we hadn't traveled down a road and back again.

Flashing back to my track days, I ran up to her room in record speed because I knew this had to be a joke. There was no way she would have really left without taking all that shit I'd bought for her over the past few weeks. I looked around once more noticing that the usual few books that she always had lying around were missing, a telltale sign that this was for real.

I still didn't want to believe it though so I dropped to the floor in the pushup position to check underneath the bed where I knew she kept her book suitcases. There was nothing there but dust bunnies and my fallen jaw. Her words from the day she'd moved in bounced around in my head and it all made sense.

But I do prefer to travel light. Always had to.

She really was gone.

But as stunned as I was somehow I still managed to make it to work like normal, but absolutely nothing got done that day. I had Neal to cancel every meeting and phone conference I had scheduled because every half hour I was calling her, but I never got an answer and after a few days, the line was disconnected altogether.

For weeks I checked my bank account several times a day to see if she had deposited or cashed the check I'd given her, but she never did. Over and over, I replayed the last twenty four hours we had spent together trying to pinpoint where exactly things had gone wrong. I narrowed it down to that first kiss and not taking the time to really talk to her before I'd left that morning because maybe I could have prevented this.

It made me chuckle bitterly when I remembered her spending time with Keith that morning because she was saying goodbye to her. She had actually said goodbye to the damn dog but not to me. But I was supposed to believe that she liked me? Yeah right. Women were even more confusing than I thought before I met her.

Wait that was it! Keith. It suddenly clicked that she should've been back working at PetWorld by now especially since she hadn't spent the money she'd gotten from me. I called to see if she was in for the day yet on a Saturday, but I was told that she no longer worked there. I asked if she had returned from the break she took for her "grandmother's death" and I was told that no one had heard from her so she'd been terminated.

When I ended the call I felt empty and alone and more worried than I thought possible. She had filled my head with so many depressing statistics of missing black women and girls that I wondered if she had become one of them.

Had she fallen asleep somewhere? Had somebody hurt her? Was she dead? Why wouldn't she just let me know that she was okay even if she was leaving?

The police were no help when I went down to my local precinct so every night before bed I asked myself those questions before I decided to use the limited information that I had to find her myself. The first stop was the motel I had found her in. The manager hadn't seen her, but I left a cash incentive for him and my card if she showed up. I knew she didn't really have any friends or family, but she had mentioned in passing that her hair braider worked with her at Bean so I tracked her down because I figured she had put them back in now.

Unfortunately she hadn't heard from Amber either so I begrudgingly went looking for Gareth because maybe she had gone to stay with him. I didn't have a last name on him, but I knew there couldn't have been too many niggas running around with that name in the tristate area. Turns out it was five, but that wasn't important. I lied and told him that I was her cousin trying to get in touch with her about our grandmother, but his shrimpy ass had the same story as the braider and said that he hadn't actually seen her since the top of the year.

Amber really had disappeared and it was almost like she had never been there at all. If it wasn't for the closet full of new stuff I could have convinced myself that I had dreamed her up, but that tight feeling in my chest and groin when I thought about her reminded me that she was not a mirage.

I was so desperate for clues about her whereabouts that I even finally got around to reading the book she'd left for me, but there was nothing in there but stories about men who were just as broken as I was finally getting their shit together. The spine was damaged and the pages were already tattered when I had first started it, but by my forth read the thing had literally fallen apart in my hands and I couldn't help but compare my short-lived relationship with the text to the one that I'd had with her.

For a while I wondered if hiring somebody to find her would be going too far. I mean it wasn't like she was my girlfriend for real and I had only known her a month. Literally thirty fucking days.

Still fucking vanishing in this day and age was weird as hell. And I mean I would have expected it if she had like scammed me or stolen something out of my place, but not even taking the shit I'd gotten for her or spending the money said more than my ears wanted to hear.

It said that there was no point in looking for her because she didn't want to be...no, wouldn't be found.

At least not by me anyway.

7

SLEEP LIKE A BABY

Months passed and the memories of Amber grew just as distant as her actual physical being was to me. The month of August came and went without warning, but I didn't even bother celebrating my birthday this year because I'd wanted to ease into my third decade not face plant into it.

Before my born day had always symbolized just another trip around the sun for me, but at least last year I was content with how I was living.

I had been generally fine with how my life was before, but now that I knew better, *knew her*, I couldn't just go back to how it used to be no matter how hard I tried to. At first I thought bringing different women home again would help me forget about her, but I still didn't want them in my bed and I definitely didn't want them in her room now either because just like with my dad's stuff, I still hadn't been able to get rid of what she'd left behind.

Sometimes I went in there and tried to remember what it looked like before she had invaded my space with her icy warmth, but I couldn't anymore because this was no longer just a spare bedroom. It belonged to her now and if at any point she wanted to come back to it then she could, no questions asked.

Looking back at everything the signs were there. In those last couple weeks she had started leaning a little closer when I was speaking and holding onto my hand a little tighter. It had become real to her too and much sooner than she'd admitted to me, but I didn't see it until it was too late to do anything about it.

Keith had been moping around since she'd left too and I felt like shit for running off her friend, but I felt even worse for running off mine because I missed everything about her. I missed her laugh. I missed her cooking. I missed her just being there when I got up. I missed roasting each other. I missed her randomly waking me up when she couldn't get to sleep then her falling while I stayed up and watched her.

I missed everything about what had become the most memorable and chaotic, but fun month of my life. And I wished that somehow I could end up in a time loop with us reliving the whole thing again and again until I got it right because even getting it wrong with her still felt better than everything I'd had before her.

This was the kind of love that my dad and my Gram used to warn me about. The kind that snuck up on you. And the real truth was that I was so scared to let anybody in out of fear of losing them how my dad had lost my mother, but each of the thirty days that I had spent with Amber had me unintentionally doing just that. She was inside of me like a motherfucker.

And now I realized that she hadn't been training me for one of those women in the catalog. Those women would have been fine with me just the way I was. But Amber had made me into the right man for herself because most women couldn't care less that I knew black feminist theory now. And she had been proud to see me be able to quote and contextualize Walker, hooks, Lorde and Davis the same way I knew how to effortlessly make pitchbooks at work. But I knew it was all for nothing now because it had all been for her and thanks to me, there would never be an *us*.

Gram didn't like the backsliding she'd seen in me over the past few months and she wasn't shy about vocalizing it. Because of that I didn't want to be around her so I told her that I'd been working weekends and arranged for a driver to take her to church on Sundays now.

I couldn't get away from her today though because it was Thanksgiving and this year it just so happened to be falling on her birthday. Since it was her ninetieth we were supposed to be going all out, but I left all the planning to Cam and Chase but volunteered my place to have it so I wouldn't look too bad to Gram.

When I got up that morning, Chase was already here and almost done cooking, but I didn't even bother volunteering to help with the rest because I wasn't in the *being alive* spirit let alone the holiday spirit since I didn't have shit to feel thankful for.

I was still in a weird space with Cam and we hadn't talked since the wedding, but I went and picked him and Tillar up from the airport a little after noon because she was pretty far along in her pregnancy now and I didn't want my new niece or nephew coming out already hating me too.

When we got back to my place all the food was done and the holiday and birthday decorations were put up, but Chase was nowhere to be found because he had left to go get Parker and her son so that they could celebrate with us.

I guess with all the talk of selling dad's house, Tillar wanted to see it while it was still in the family so Cam decided to take her since Gram still hadn't arrived. I'd thought that I would be picking her up too, but she let me know that

Deacon Johnson was visiting today so he would bring her up after. I didn't even have it in me to tease her about her little boyfriend so I just agreed with the change of plans.

When she did finally get to my place, Gram was impressed by the feast that Chase had prepared by himself because in the past we always did it as a family. She'd instructed him to at least save the pies for last so that she could make them with him, but he wasn't answering when we called so she asked me to help her instead. I wasn't really in the mood to, but my spirits lifted some after putting on a dusties radio station and peeling sweet potatoes with her because it made me think about how so little had changed from when I was complaining about doing this as a kid.

All the pies were in the oven and since Gram wouldn't let me have any of the food until everybody got back, I decided to snack on the leftover graham cracker crusts that we'd made. After throwing the last few crumbs in my mouth, I got a text from Cam letting me know that while they were looking around the house a woman named Amber had shown up and she claimed to know me.

I didn't know which one fell faster, the bowl I'd been holding or my phone, but both hit the ground in a loud thud which startled Gram who had been watching the Thanksgiving Day Parade on TV.

She asked me what was wrong, but I had no time to explain because I knew I had to get there before Amber left with no breadcrumbs to find her again. Gram asked where I was going in such a hurry so I told her that I had finally tracked Amber down at dad's house.

"Wait. Before you go--" she began, but I zoomed past her out the door. I had gotten over to the elevator when I realized that Chase still had my set of keys for our dad's house so Amber couldn't have gotten in that way like I'd assumed. There were only four sets of keys to the old house. Chase had both his and mine and Cam had just used his to let himself in so that only left one set.

"Gram, how did Amber get in the house?" I asked straightforwardly as I came back inside the apartment.

"Well I-I..." she began then let her words trail off. And for as long as I had been alive I had never seen my grandmother at a loss for words so I knew that my sudden hunch was correct. She was in on this.

"Gram, how could you do this to me when you knew that I had been looking for her? That I thought she might be dead!" I shouted at her for the first time ever, but I didn't regret it because she had earned that little piece of disrespect.

"Now hold up, Christian Alexander Logan. I love you with everything inside of me, but you have more in common with your late grandfather than even I like to admit sometimes. I might be able to look the other way and still love you for who you are because I raised you, but Amber doesn't owe you that. She deserves more and if you're not going to be the man that we all know you're capable of being, then don't go over there and interfere with her plans," she said before she suddenly stopped speaking at the realization of what she'd let slip out.

"Her plans for what?" I asked angrily.

"Well I think it would be best if I let her tell you."

"Oh so now you know how to keep secrets, huh? You've been gossiping about everybody your whole life, but when it comes to me you suddenly know how to keep it zipped? Any way you look at it, that's messed up, Gram, and you know it!" I said in frustration in her direction before leaving out.

I finally found something to be thankful for, but it was just that I had already given Cam my car to use because my head wasn't clear enough to drive anyway. I decided to hail a taxi and for the first time in my life it didn't take a decade for it to happen.

I didn't know what I was expecting to see

when I walked inside my dad's house, but it sure wasn't Cam, Tillar and Amber sitting in the kitchen eating chopped cheese sandwiches like they were the best of friends. I knew that smell anywhere though because Cam and Chase were crazy about those heart attacks on a hoagie since we were kids, but I was always partial to the baconeggandcheese.

Thanks to their loud laughter, I had successfully crept into the living room without being detected so I stood quietly in place and listened to some of their conversation before I decided how to proceed with Amber.

"So how far along are you?" I heard Amber ask Tillar.

"Cam, how many months ago was the honeymoon?"

"Seven months," he answered with a mouthful of food.

"Seven months then," she joked and they all laughed. "What about you? When are you due?" she asked Amber and if I wasn't already leaning on the wall, I would have fallen flat on my face because...what the fuck?

"End of March, but I'm hoping to induce because I really don't want to bring another Aries girl into this world," she responded before Tillar got play offended.

"Hey I'm an April Aries and we are not that

bad!"

"Really? My fault. My grandmother ruined all of y'all for me."

"Say no more. My mother is a Taurus and I side-eye the whole damn sign because of her too," Tillar began, but I couldn't just stay out there anymore and I had to make my presence known.

"Sorry to break up all the useless zodiac talk, but can somebody please tell me what the fuck is going on here?"

At the sound of my voice Cam got up and walked over to me. He tried to get me to go to the living room so we could talk alone for a minute, but nothing he had to say was more important than me seeing Amber Miller sitting at the table where I had dinner as a kid with a protruding belly.

"Whatever it is can wait. You've been here this whole time, Amber? And pregnant? Why would you go behind my back and get my Gram involved in your shit?" I asked her raising my voice because I was already upset at Gram and I couldn't pretend like I wasn't mad at her too even though I was grateful that she was still alive and unharmed.

Well almost unharmed because that baby had ballooned her up and her face had gotten a little chubby. It was still cute though, but I had to make myself forget about that for now because she had been dumb enough to let a nigga named Gareth knock her up. And clearly he didn't want shit to do with her anymore once shit got real which was why she had resorted to asking Gram to stay here.

"No I've only been here the last couple months. The doctors said I couldn't take my medicine like this and without it I couldn't work anymore so your grandmother said I could stay here until she's born. And please don't be upset at her because I begged her not to tell you," she said as Cam and Tillar left to give us a minute alone to talk.

"And just where do you plan on going next with a little ass baby and no job and no savings, huh? You can barely stay awake and take care of yourself. How do you think you're gonna be able to do this on your own?" I asked her because these were things she should have thought about before fucking that broke nigga raw.

"Chris, I'm not keeping her," she said softly and lowered her head.

All of a sudden I felt like an idiot when I finally thought about how far along she was. If she was due in March like she had just told Tillar then that meant that there was a possibility that the baby could be mine. But it couldn't be because we had literally only had sex that one time and we had used a condom. But then... aw fuck.

Obviously I was no fool and I knew how shit worked, but there was no way in hell that this shit could be happening to me. I swallowed the big gulp of spit that had been collecting in my wide open mouth for the last minute or so because I knew that I had to ask her a difficult and incredibly uncomfortable question.

"Amber, is she mine? Is that why Gram let you stay here?" I asked and surprised even myself when my voice went higher than normal.

She slowly nodded yes to both questions then volunteered that she knew for sure that the baby was mine because she always used protection with Gareth and the dates wouldn't have lined up anyway because she hadn't been with him since New Year's Day which reminded me that he had said the same thing when I had asked him months ago.

I took a couple deep breaths and tried to keep my composure, but that woosah shit just wouldn't cut it today.

Today I needed to yell and shout about how fucked up it was that she would do this to me and keep me in the dark about something as important as having a baby on the way. And then on top of everything she had apparently just decided to give her away because her wannabe feminist ass was pro-choice for everybody else, but yet she couldn't take care of this before letting it get this far along.

"Can you please just calm down?" she asked me to no avail.

"Fuck no! You don't get to keep something like this from me then expect me to be calm. I was so fucking worried about your ass all this time, Amber. I thought you could be dead and I blamed myself for that so much that I even wanted to--" I began but stopped myself from talking about my own suicidal thoughts because I didn't want to give her any ideas while she was carrying my child. "But see this is what I'm talking about with you women wanting your cake, your cookies and your fucking brownies and to eat them too! Y'all get to be the most selfish, entitled motherfuckers at a time like this and you call it feminism, but when I act entitled then I'm an incel, right?"

"Yeah and what about it? I've put up with so much shit from you from all angles Chris that I deserve all the fucking desserts Betty Crocker can make!" she yelled back at me as she started to cry uncontrollably. It hurt me to see her like that, but comforting her was the last thing on my mind because after learning about all of this I needed to be fucking comforted too.

"Well have at it then, but you're not giving my baby away. If you don't want to be a mother fine, but you're not keeping me from being a dad!" I told her angrily because she had another thing coming if she thought that I wouldn't drag her ass to court for full custody of my seed.

I might not have been shit as a boyfriend or future husband, but I would never understand men who knew they had kids out there and didn't take care of them. Literally the instant she had said that baby was mine, I felt a kinship with her and I hadn't even gotten a damn DNA test yet.

When Cam heard me raising my voice at her, he came and collected me from the kitchen and brought me out to the old backyard where we used to throw the ball around while our dad manned the grill. It took a while of trying to get through to me, but he convinced me to go back home and cool off for now and then he promised to come back with me tomorrow and to help facilitate a discussion how he'd planned to today before I got here and fucked everything up.

Tillar must've had a similar conversation with Amber because when we came back inside she had stopped crying and they were now hugging to the best of their abilities because their bellies only allowed them to do it from the side. Amber looked away when she saw me and I swear that simple gesture broke my heart into a million pieces because all I had wanted for months now was for her to see me and realize that she loved me too, but now it was looking like that would never happen. And as much as I wanted to place the blame on her, I knew that the way I'd treated her was the real culprit.

"So what are you gonna do?" Cam asked me after he had helped Tillar into the passenger seat of the car and arranged the seatbelt around her belly.

"I'm gonna step up and raise my daughter," I said annoyed at him because it should have been obvious.

"I know that. The Logan men are honorable," he said sounding just like our dad. "But what about her?"

"What about her? She doesn't want to be involved and I can't force her so I'll do it by myself." I said confidently because if my dad could successfully raise three boys without a mother, then surely I could do alright with one little girl.

"Don't you think there's something else you could do to change her mind?" he asked trying to blame me for her actions, but I wasn't going for that. I accepted responsibility for my part, but leaving and hiding the pregnancy from me was still all on her because I would have welcomed her back at any time.

"Man fuck you! She left and she kept this from me. I'm not wrong here. And I'm not letting her give my baby away."

"Okay genius, do you know how long a

custody suit is gonna take? Take it from me, Chris. You don't want to be separated from your child for any amount of time let alone forever," he said as he looked at me through the rear view mirror. "Do you want to be right or do you want to be happy?"

"I am happy."

"Right. I can tell because it's all rainbows and sunshine back there," he remarked sarcastically before Tillar put her hand on his knee and whispered for him to be nicer to me. He sighed and gripped the steering wheel tighter then tried a new approach to get through to me.

"Chris, remember when you asked me about Ashley before the wedding?" he asked and it surprised me that he would bring up his ex-girlfriend because Tillar was right there. She didn't even flinch though and continued scrolling on her phone.

"Yeah. You blew me off about it."

"Well what I should've told you was that we broke up because I wasn't ready for her because I still wasn't over losing Summer and Cree yet. But when I saw Tillar, I realized that I would never really be ready, but I knew I had met somebody so special that it didn't matter because I wasn't letting her get away," he said as he began to slow down for the upcoming yellow light.

"How did you know?" I asked and hated

how painfully naïve I sounded, but I honestly just had never concerned myself with matters of the heart much because it seemed pointless. "How did you know that it wasn't just lust or loneliness anymore? That it was the real thing?" I asked because in spite of my strong feelings for Amber, I didn't want to believe that love was as tough as this situation had been.

"It's a cliché, but you really do just know. Instantly she was my weakness. I loved having her around, but more importantly I noticed the difference whenever she left and that's when I knew for sure," he said as he put one hand on her belly then began driving again with the other. And for the first time ever, his words actually resonated with me because it felt like he was describing how I felt about Amber. "Nobody makes me laugh like she does and when she looks at me I forget to breathe sometimes. I wasn't expecting to meet somebody like her when I did, but I got ready for her."

Then like he was reading my mind he asked, "Do you feel any of that with Amber?" I sighed then slowly nodded as I wiped a loose tear away before anybody saw it. "Then fight for her too, Chris. Not just the baby."

"I will," I said for my own ears to hear moreso than his.

"Good. And don't go pressing Gram about

this again or I'll show you that my hands still work," he threatened me and I had a good chuckle about it.

The first thing I did when I came back in was found Gram and apologized to her. But despite the good brotherly talk I'd just had with Cam I was still mad at everybody but mostly at myself because it was suddenly hitting me that I had missed months of doctor's appointments and backaches and foot rubs. While everybody else was sitting around and enjoying the music and their cake, I was finally accepting that all I wanted was a brownie and my baby and my Amber. And I didn't care what name I would be called for it. I would do whatever she asked to be the man she wrapped her arms around at night.

I knew something was up with Chase when he showed back up late and without Parker and her kid, but I was in my head too much to even ask what was going on. Plus this was the first time that he and Cam had seen each other since he'd missed the wedding so I knew some bullshit was bound to happen. Gram must have felt the same way because she tried her best to keep him in good spirits, but it turned out that he didn't have a problem with Cam today. It was with me.

"This is probably the last time we'll all be together until next year this time so let's just put everything on the table about the house," Chase began before Cam looked over at me.

"Actually, let's hold off on that for a little bit, alright? You just got here. Have some cake," Cam suggested before getting Tillar settled in her seat and I felt a pang of jealousy because I was missing out on that and more with Amber. I couldn't even focus on the party let alone a conversation about the house so I just picked over my slice and prepared for their incoming argument.

"I don't want any cake," Chase said sounding like a kid. "And hold off for what? Just last night you said we were going to convince Chris today."

"I know what I said, but things change so let's drop it," Cam said putting some bass in his voice.

"What changed from last night?" Chase asked waiting around for a good explanation.

"Me and Tillar went there today and we decided that we might use it when we come up here to see Gram," Cam said lying on my behalf. I knew how much he hated it, but just like when he fought my bullies, he had done it because he loved me.

Now admittedly I was in and out of the conversation after that, but even half listening I still didn't know how they managed to end up on those damn records again.

"Nigga you don't even have a record player! You just don't want me to have them!" Cam shouted at Chase.

"I would've bought one if he gave them to me."

"But he only gave them to me because I collected my own."

"I didn't want my own. I wanted what we grew up listening to."

"But you don't see me asking you to ship me the Bluebird to drive for part of the year or for Chris to let me borrow one of dad's watches so why should I have to split what he left me with y'all?" Cam asked but was met with silence.

He was right too, but it was beyond the records at this point because we had both resented him for being the favorite all of our lives. But lately I didn't even care about any of that petty shit anymore. Gram was taken care of and the money and properties were split three ways and that was all that mattered so I told them that and for once I felt like the most mature brother.

"Look I'mma just say it since nobody else will, Chase. If you need money that bad then I'll write you a check, but we're not putting up the house," Cam said definitively which caused Chase to lose it because neither of us or Gram had ever had the guts to mention how concerned we were with how much trust money he'd blown on his failed restaurants.

"Yo fuck you! This shit ain't about money," he claimed defensively, but Cam didn't look convinced and honestly neither did I, but I tried to remain neutral. "Like it or not, I'm my own man and I went my own way, failures and all. Niggas like you want people to think you're self-made, but you're anything but. And it's not my fault that you're obsessed with the real Cam Logan and trying to live his life all over again instead of living your own. You're running shops like him. Hell you even got a dead wife like him," Chase angrily spat and I just knew Cam was about to put it on him so I backed out of the way lest I get hit with a stray fist, but to my surprise my oldest brother just calmly took a deep breath then left the room.

I knew Chase could hold his own in a fight, but he didn't know how lucky he was that Tillar was present because I could still feel those punches that I was given months ago. Tillar went to check on Cam and Gram tried to intervene and make Chase go apologize, but he was still upset and ranting about everything so she finally just asked him to leave if he couldn't calm himself down. Of course this angered him even more and he accused her of choosing Cam's side over his.

Finally I had to step in and tell him that there were more important matters going on right now and that this petty bullshit would have to wait. He then tried to get loud with me, but I stood to my feet to let him know that he wasn't about to raise his voice at me in my house. I had too much shit running through my mind and I would hate to take it out on him, but I would if he took me there.

When he finally realized that he had nobody in his corner today, not even me, he grabbed his shit and stormed out, almost running into somebody that was standing in the hallway about to knock. Gram gasped immediately, but it took me a full ten seconds to realize that it wasn't just somebody.

It was Amber.

After seeing her very pregnant belly Chase looked back at me and shook his head before going around her and leaving out. Amber stood in place for a while looking around at all the decorations and food before she spoke.

"I'm sorry. I didn't know you were having a get-together today so I'll come back some other time," she said softly, but before she could turn on her heels Gram was already inviting her all the way in to have a seat. Keith immediately ran over and excitedly jumped all over her. I doubted that her paws could actually hurt anything, but instinctively I went to calm her down before she touched Amber's belly. But just like before Amber told me she could handle her and they got reunited as Keith slobbered all over her.

It was at that exact time that Cam and Tillar joined us again and at the sight of Amber there, I heard Tillar curse under her breath because this day just would not let up on the drama. After that all eyes were on me and waiting to see what my next move would be, but to be honest I didn't know what to say or do. I was hurt and confused, but I also knew that I had hurt and confused Amber too so after a couple minutes of nobody saying a word, I blurted out what I wanted her to know first.

"I'm not gonna let you go through this alone anymore. I want to be there for you and the baby so I'm gonna do the right thing," I assured her before very practically suggesting that we should get married so that she could be added on my insurance and figure out what to do about her medicine. But as it turned out, me being practical at a time like this wasn't received well.

"No. That's not why I came here, Chris. That's not what I want," she said angrily as she got up to go for the door, but I got there before she could and stood in front of it because now I was upset again.

"What do you want then? You left me without warning and then you show up pregnant expecting me to have all the answers! Do *you* even know what the hell you want at this point?!" I repeated yelling at her and disregarding that we were having this conversation in front of an audience.

"I wanted you to ask me to stay!" she yelled back so loud that it seemed to echo across the walls.

"Are you crazy?! I did ask you to stay! More than fucking once, I asked you Amber!" I shouted then reminded her how she had turned me down every single time.

"No, you asked me to be your chef, your maid, even your damn dog walker. Everything but your partner, Chris! How do you think that made me feel after finally admitting to myself that I was falling in love with you?" she asked then stopped speaking because her voice was beginning to crack from emotion. I didn't know whether to be happy to hear her confirm her feelings for me or mad that she hadn't said any of this before she left so I said nothing until a cute thought came into my head.

"Well I'm sorry, but in all fairness wives all over the world cook, clean and walk dogs every day, B," I mocked her trying to bring some levity to the tense conversation, but apparently it was the wrong move.

"Since this is all still a game to you, how about you and the half-assed marriage you're offering me can both go to hell because I don't want either one," she said trying to push passed me, but I told her I wasn't letting her leave until we came to a mutual decision about what to do.

Out of nowhere Gram raised her voice and instructed me to get out of the way, but I didn't listen because her meddling had already caused enough trouble and I could handle things from here.

Just wanting to get away from me for a moment, a highly annoyed Amber sighed then headed for the main terrace, but she must've been more exhausted than she seemed because she nearly fainted before she could get there. Luckily she was within arm's reach of Cam because his quick reflexes allowed him to catch her before she could hit the floor.

Tillar instantly panicked and began calling for an ambulance before I explained that she was narcoleptic and this kind of thing happened sometimes. After checking to make sure her breathing was stable, Cam carried her over to her old bedroom. Gram followed after him, but she was clearly so disappointed that she refused to even look at me.

With just me and Tillar in it now, the room was once again quiet, but that didn't mean i didn't feel the intense judgement coming from the other side of the couch we shared.

"What? You can't say I didn't at least try, right?" I asked nervously chuckling because I was still trying to wrap my mind around how things had gone so wrong so fast in so many ways today.

"You call that trying?" Tillar asked as she looked at me clearly unimpressed at my performance here today, but I didn't see what I had done that was so bad. I was just trying to look at things logically since everybody's emotions were on ten.

"Okay you're into fairytales and shit like that. What would Prince Charming do to fix this?"

"Well for one Prince Charming wouldn't have gotten himself in a situation like this, but then again you aren't exactly Prince Charming, are you? You're more like Duke of the Damned," she quipped, but I wasn't in the mood to be poked at and I was sure it showed on my face.

"Alright unfortunately, I don't think there is a quick fix for this situation, Chris, but you can start by telling her how you really feel then being consistent if she lets you back in. I can tell you really love her and it has nothing to do with the baby so just go tell her that."

"And what if she still says no?"

"Then you'll just have to accept her decision, but there's a good chance she might give you one more chance if you try a real proposal and didn't make marrying you sound about as exciting as a Pap smear. You know, where you know you have to do it, but you just don't want to," she said as she playfully bumped my shoulder with hers. For the first time, I really looked at her and took in all of her beauty and grace and that pregnancy glow certainly looked nice on her too.

"I see why he loves you so much," I told her honestly. "I never said anything out loud, but I've thought some pretty fucked up shit about you and I'm really sorry about that."

"That's okay. You don't even wanna know all the real shit I've talked about you and Chase for almost ruining my wedding," she told me with a grin.

"Well I can't speak for Chase, but I'm sorry for how I acted that weekend and I'll do better going forward because we're officially dropping the in-law from our title. You're just my sister now."

"Aw thank you, but we're still not inviting y'all to anything else," she said and I laughed out loud for the first time in what felt like an eternity.

"Oh I'm coming and I promise I'll act right," I said as I leaned over to kiss her cheek and hug her tightly. Cam must have sensed that another man had his hands on her because he came out and broke that shit up immediately.

"That's enough of that. Go get your own wife, baby brother," he told me warmly before I stood to my feet and looked up at him.

In that moment I realized that it wasn't about the few extra inches he had on me in height or the fact that he had my dad's name. He was just the better man because he had conviction and he embraced his emotions instead of burying them like I had done my whole life. And in two years' time when I would be his age now, I wanted nothing more than to be half the man he was. And if it meant I was a follower then so be it because there was nobody better to be led by.

"Chris you know I've been here before," Cam began about the fact that he too was once faced with marrying a scared girl after he had gotten her pregnant, "but I have a feeling that you can learn from my mistakes and create a better outcome than I did," he said sincerely before opening up his arms to me.

I hesitated for a second because I couldn't remember the last time I'd hugged another man period let alone my brother. But when we connected it felt like he was passing the official "welcome to real manhood" torch to me and I wholeheartedly accepted it as tears began to fall from my weary eyes.

I cried because I realized that even though there were a few parallels to Cam's relationship with Summer and mine with Amber, it was still different because doing the right thing here just so happened to be everything that I never knew I wanted. Nobody else would ever get to see the real me like she had and she'd still stupidly wanted me anyway. If that wasn't love then I didn't know what was.

I let Cam go then took long steps to get back to Amber faster. I stood in the doorway and watched Gram by her side watching over her as she slept. When she saw me she rose to her feet.

"I'm gonna try to make it right, Gram, but no matter what she decides, I'm gonna be the kind of man that you can be proud of," I promised her as I kissed her cheek then closed the door after her so that we could have some privacy when Amber woke up again.

With all of this talk of princes and fairytales with Tillar, I chuckled to myself about how I'd somehow stumbled upon my own personal little Harlem, feminist version of Sleeping Beauty. But instead of kissing Amber awake this time, I patiently waited until she began to move and I let her get up in her own time. Her eyes began to get wet when she saw that it was me lying next to her, but I spoke before I lost the courage to put myself at the mercy of being rejected by her again.

"I should've said this before, months ago even, but I'll say it now because it's still true. I love you, Amber, and I want you to stay. And I know it won't be easy to be with me, but I'll do what needs to be done to get us where we need to be. And I promise I'll wash all the dishes and I'll even cook too and I'll read more feminist books with you. I'll do it all and I'll love it because it'll mean that I get to be with you," I told her before taking a deep breath because I had just given her everything I had in me.

"You're just saying this because you're still competing with Cam, right? What, you think we can just skip over all the work they put in but magically have what they have?"

"No, because I don't want what they have. I want what we had but better because I'll be better now," I pleaded with her and even though she looked like she didn't believe me I still went on. "I'm not competing with Cam anymore, but I do want to be happy like him and you made me happy from the start. The first kiss we shared that day in the park didn't just wake you up. It woke me up too and I wish I could go back and do everything right, but I can't. I can start over today though and give you all of me if you say you want me too."

Always a woman of many words, I was stunned to see her willingly being silent, but after waiting for an eternity for her to say something, I decided to keep speaking from my soul and hoping that it reached hers.

"Amber, how many times have you called

me stupid since we met? It had to be at least a hundred, right? And it's true because I am stupid for not telling you how I felt sooner and for letting you get away. I admit that everything I've ever said to you was wrong. I was wrong about women, about you and about me. I wasn't an incel because I hated women. I was an incel because I hated myself, but you taught me how to love myself, Amber and that's how I know that I love you." She finally sighed before looking over at me.

"Chris, I don't know if I ever want to get married at all, but I know for sure that I don't want a shotgun marriage," she said and it was my turn to sigh because I didn't care about that superficial shit. I just wanted her.

"How is it a shotgun though when I want to marry you?"

"Did the definition suddenly change? You were not thinking about getting married to me before finding out I was pregnant today."

"Well not exactly, but I knew I wanted you in my life and that's why I've been going crazy looking for you all this time. And thinking about us getting married and having a kid is scary as fuck, but scary in a good way because not many people get to go through something like this with their best friend. C'mon you know you're my only friend and I mean technically we've already been married from day one anyway," I reminded her of how we pretended to be together for the police officer and she lightly chuckled.

While I had her smiling, I decided that it was now or never so I dropped down on one knee to give her the type of proposal that she deserved. I didn't have a ring on me, but I would get her the nicest one money could buy once she agreed to put up with me for the rest of our lives. I took the most precious thing that I owned, my dad's favorite watch, and placed it on her small wrist.

"Amber Miller, I love you and I want to be with you for as long as you'll have me. I should have known that you were the one for me from the very beginning when I wanted to help you because I've never wanted to help anybody a day in my life," I said in all seriousness as another stream of tears began rolling down my face, but she thought it was funny as she wiped them for me.

"But how do I know that this isn't just temporary? Why should I say yes?"

"Because…" I began trying to think of something perfect to say that would convince her, but I decided that the truth was much better. "Because just like you, I still don't know what I believe in, God, heaven or whatever. But for the first time in my life I prayed for something. I prayed for you. And there has to be something magical up there because it brought me to you in the first place, right? You loving me is proof that there's somebody up there, Amber. So please make my day and say that you'll marry me and that we'll raise our daughter together. Please," I begged her with no shame as I laid my head on her stomach, but she was quiet again for what felt like the longest few minutes of my life.

I knew that couldn't be a good omen so I held on tighter knowing that this might be my last chance to do this, but finally she picked my head up and looked me in the eyes as she spoke.

"Chris, you've been a nonstop nuisance since the day I met you," she began and I lowered my head expecting another rejection until she went on, "so I guess I shouldn't have been surprised to find out that your sperm was just as annoying and determined to bug me for the rest of my life too," she said as she smiled through a few tears of her own.

"So you are gonna keep her then?" I asked still unsure if that's what she meant and she nodded. "And you're gonna marry me too, aren't you?"

"Yes. Your biggest incel fear has officially come true. I'm gonna marry you for your money," she said, but I was still grinning from ear to ear because I knew she was lying.

"No, you actually love me too, don't you?" I asked and she groaned then bit her lip.

"I wish I didn't."

"I know and I plan on doing everything in my power to change that starting now. I want to be a different person with you. I want to raise a family and just be simple with you."

"But you don't like simple, remember? You want the lights and the fancy dinners."

"Being simple with you will be the most remarkable shit that's ever happened to me. And I'm still taking you to a nice restaurant even if I have to carry you there every now and then. I won't even get mad at you for looking at the menu before because marriage is about compromise, right?" I joked as she touched the bags that had formed under my eyes again.

"How have you been sleeping without me?"

"Not much. I thought my rem cycles were off before you, but trying to sleep with a broken heart these last few months was one of the hardest things I've ever done and I never want to do it again."

"You won't have to," she said as she cradled my head in her arms.

And all at once I felt the greatest sense of relief and also like I had just moved a mountain. It'd probably never happen again in this lifetime so I let myself fall asleep before her as I soothingly rubbed her stomach.

And as I drifted off I thought about how

unfortunate it was that up until this point I had given her one of those dark Grimm Brothers' fairytales, but from here on out I would make it my mission to create one that even Disney couldn't top.

♕

Making the decision to move back into my dad's house wasn't very hard when I realized that Amber had gotten used to living there and preferred it over the penthouse. And being there with her made it feel like home again to the point that I knew I would never live the high rise life again. But I didn't think anybody loved it as much as Keith did because she had free reign over the backyard until we added two new dogs, Johnny Gill and Gerald Levert, to the family in order to create the canine LSG.

Admittedly I was OD overprotective during the rest of the pregnancy and I swear I would have wrapped Amber in bubble wrap if she let me, but just staying close by me was enough for her to feel safe and it made me feel like a real man for the first time in my life.

Her pregnancy was pretty high risk for a number of reasons so she mostly stayed in which made me take it upon myself to make home fun for her. I cut my work hours almost in half and we played all the board games, watched all the movies, and read all the books that she had missed throughout her less than fortunate childhood. And it made me happy seeing her smile and knowing that once again she was experiencing something for the first time with me.

It wasn't all fun and games though. The moment we got settled we decided to have a therapist come by twice a week to keep us on the same page of this new age fairytale we were living. Of course we were already doing a much better job communicating and we were committed to staying together, but there was nothing like having a professional around to help make the ride less bumpy. We loved each other with everything we had, but we both recognized that love wasn't always enough with two people as complicated as us.

She was raised to survive not thrive and I'd never felt worthy of genuine love which was why I'd never given it to anybody before her. But we were bettering ourselves so that our baby girl wouldn't have to be on some shrink's couch in twenty years healing from damage caused by us.

But even under the unconventional circumstances and her tiredness, overall Amber had a pretty easy last trimester. Out of nowhere she would even have a little boost in energy sometimes due to her hormones. The baby was healthy and hitting all of her milestones on time, but I was still worried about the actual birthing process and possible complications because of my own mother. I tried to keep my mind off of negativity though and I focused on all the good that had been going on.

When it came time to pick a name, I was not the least bit surprised when my very feminist wife suggested making our daughter a junior and I didn't fight it at all. The wait was officially on for bad ass Amber Chanel Miller-Logan Jr. to be born, but we had just been calling her AJ for short and I liked it.

But my anxiety went through the roof when AJ decided to surprise us and come earlier than expected at thirty weeks. I didn't want Amber to feel my nervous energy in the delivery room so I took a drink to relax so that I could be by her side, but she was surprisingly fine during the whole thing. She had an epidural and actually somehow slept through most of it after working herself up a little towards the last contractions. The doctors had never seen anything like it, but I knew how deep her sleep spells could be so nothing surprised me anymore. I was just overjoyed to present her with my mini me when she woke up again.

"She's got my name, but she already looks

just like you, Chris. A whole copy and paste job. What the hell?" she complained to me, but I couldn't wipe the smile from my face.

"Don't worry. You'll show up later, but in the meantime look at what we made," I said proudly before I kissed the top of both their heads.

"*We*?" she asked pointing at the ice pack on her lower half.

"Okay technically *you* made her, but I helped," I joked before getting serious. "You ready to hold her?"

She nodded, but I could see that she was scared to because of her cataplexy so after placing AJ in her arms, I wrapped mine around her to let her know that I had them both and I wouldn't ever let anything bad happen to them.

And I wasn't even ashamed of the fact that I probably cried more than AJ that day when it finally hit me that I was officially a dad. Because despite not listening to most of his words of wisdom until the past year, I revered my dad more than any other man that had walked this earth so I would definitely be taking my new role just as seriously as he had.

I remembered foolishly thinking in my younger years that having a daughter would be karma dishing out a serving of humble pie to me, but now I knew that it was my duty to protect her and try to make the world a better place for her to live in.

I had already planned to take paternity leave for a few months to be there for Amber and AJ, but a couple weeks at home with them full time had me putting in my official resignation with Reisman because I knew I wouldn't be returning at all. The day that Neal cleared out my office and brought everything to me was a scary one, but I knew I had made the right decision for my family because my new work was at home.

If anybody would've told me a year ago that I would be married let alone a stay at home dad, I would have laughed in their faces, but it was funny how fast things could happen when you had met the right one.

Chase still couldn't believe that I didn't want her to work anymore either, but I explained that Amber had already worked too much and it was time for her to put her feet up at home with our baby and our dogs. I knew she had never really thought about what she wanted to do with her life because she had just been focused on paying bills and staying out of trouble, but I let her know that there was no amount too big to put into whatever she wanted to do if the time ever came when she got bored at home.

Even with me no longer earning the *big*, big bucks as a banker, between my inheritance and my investments, neither one of us would ever have to work again. At least not until we had found something that we truly loved and that could fit around being a family because that was the number one priority.

But because of some of his opinions I had admittedly been distancing myself from Chase anyway. Even though he seemed happy at some of the changes that I'd made, I could sense that working on my relationship with Cam wasn't one of them. I guess it had been us against him for so long that anything else felt like betrayal, but I couldn't go on like that anymore. I needed my biggest brother now more than ever because he had been through what I was going through a couple times so he was practically an expert on family life.

The new more costly medications that Amber took for her cataplexy helped a lot and seeing her be able to laugh with her whole body now even made me feel more alive. Of course there was still no cure for her overall narcoleptic condition so we were still scheduling family naps even though AJ didn't always get with the program. Amber was really worried that she would pass it down to her because of the genetic component, but I did what I could to keep those thoughts at bay for both of us. If she did have it, she would probably be a teenager before she got symptoms and knowing that we had the means to get her diagnosed and treated early instead of in her twenties like Amber was a huge comforting thought for now.

And today, Valentine's Day, had officially marked two months since we'd been married and AJ was turning one month old so we had a lot of love to celebrate this year. Amber didn't feel up to going out so I had cooked her a romantic dinner followed up by a pan of homemade brownies for dessert by the fireplace since the snowstorm outside was getting pretty bad.

All that milk I'd had with the brownies had killed my stomach and I had been on the toilet for so long that my legs were numb, but that didn't stop me from continuing to look at the few wedding pictures we had for the umpteenth time just to make sure it was still real. Amber and I had been tired that whole December day but despite being exhausted, I still insisted on going to the Justice of Peace like we'd planned because I'd been playing pretend for long enough and I was ready for her to be my partner for real.

She refused to wear white with her belly so big and all of the pictures of her were from her breasts up, but my favorite was the one that a beaming Gram had snuck of us then sent to me later. I was leaning down and talking to her stomach and I must have been saying something stupid because Amber looked annoyed at me, but I could still see the love that she had for me in her eyes. I knew that I didn't deserve the life that I had now, but I had been working hard every day to be the kind of man who did. The kind of man that I had been raised to be.

As a family, we slept a lot and I swear every time I woke up it felt like I was still dreaming because I couldn't believe that I was a husband and a dad and that I, *me*, Chris Logan, was actually happy. And my beautiful wife would let me tell everybody the story of how we officially met as me saving her life in the park that fateful morning, but we both knew the truth. She had truly been the one to save me from the destructive and meaningless life I was living before our story began.

A light rapping on the bathroom door and Amber's sleep alarm brought me out of my thoughts.

"Hurry up in there. I gotta pee and it's your turn to burp her," Amber said from the bedroom with a deep yawn. I knew she was getting tired so I told her to put the baby down as a precaution. I finished up quickly because dad duty was a twenty-four/seven job around here, but as a former banker I had been training for this position for years so I had no complaints.

Even though it still wasn't very late, I shooed LSG out of the bedroom before they tried to sleep in here because otherwise they would wake me up with their barking at some point. Johnny and Gerald left immediately, but Keith took her sweet time since she was now pregnant with her first litter. Amber and I had been taking bets on who the father was, but truthfully all I really cared about was naming three of the puppies Tony, Toni and Toné.

"Hey I was just thinking that since we didn't get to do the big wedding thing, maybe we should have a big anniversary party next year. And don't forget you still owe me a honeymoon," I said trying not to sound like I had been putting in too much thought about it even though I had. I knew she wasn't the sappy type, but just in case a small part of her did want those things I wanted to give them to her.

"That's if we make it that far. I'm divorcing you if you left the toilet seat up again," she said in all seriousness as she went in after me because she had nearly fallen in a time or two. I chuckled to myself because ironically as much as I had pushed one on Cam, I hadn't even thought of asking her to sign a prenup. I figured that if I ever messed up again to where she wanted to leave me then she would deserve every penny she got.

"Good thing I made sure to put it down just now then so we can make it to infinity and beyond," I said quoting Buzz Lightyear as I picked up a smiling, but sleepy looking AJ. She was fussy and only went to sleep these days when she was lying on one of our bare chests so I had already removed my shirt to let her get as comfortable as possible.

"Well that's if I don't die from a lack of sleep first," I yawned out at the same time as AJ and it must have been contagious because Amber wasn't too far behind with hers when she got in bed with us. "It's literally only been a month and she's already kicking our asses. No matter how many hours I get, I'm always so sleepy lately."

"Good. Join the club," she quipped making me laugh and before her head could hit the pillow she was already fast asleep. I kissed her temple and thought to myself that this was it. This was our happily or rather our *sleepily* ever after and I wouldn't want it any other way.

SLEEPING CUTIE

FOLLOW ME

Thanks for reading! If you don't want to miss out on any updates about the final installment of this series (*Trapunzel*) or other works of mine then find me on all social media platforms as TanSaidWhat.

Visit www.tanzaniaglover.com

And if the cover art took your breath away as much as it did mine, check out the talented artist Bree Douthitt! Thank you so much for bringing Sleeping Cutie to life!

THANK YOUS

I said that I was done writing dissertations to my family and friends in this section so I'll try to keep this brief especially since my love for them has remained the same since the first time I did this. But I do want to say that I feel like the luckiest person in the world to be able to go on this journey with people who genuinely love and care for me. Because of the immense amount of love and support that I receive from them, I get to do the thing I love most in the world and I'm forever grateful for it.